OTHER BOOKS IN THE SERIES

Visit **www.pjwhittlesea.com** for updates on releases.

THISTLE WITCH

ANAÏS BLUE BOOK ONE

P J WHITTLESEA

Published by Tyet Books, Amsterdam

www.tyetbooks.com

information@tyetbooks.com

ISBN 9789492523181

Cover Design by Miblart

Edited by Philip Newey and Ella Holgate

For Kyro

The road to En-dor is easy to tread
For Mother or yearning Wife.
There, it is sure, we shall meet our Dead
As they were even in life.
Earth has not dreamed of the blessing in store
For desolate hearts on the road to En-dor.

— EXCERPT FROM 'EN-DOR',
RUDYARD KIPLING, 1865–1936

BLUE

Anaïs Blue hated her name.

Not the first part. She thought the name Anaïs was kind of cool. It had something mysterious about it. It was different. It was foreign. It made her feel important. It was very close to its more common counterpart, the name Anna, but unusual enough to be special. She was secretly proud to carry the name Anaïs and completely content with being its bearer. It was the name Blue that she had a problem with.

Firstly, she hated the colour itself. She didn't think it was beautiful. She couldn't stand the sight of it and, worst of all, it was everywhere. When she looked up, it was there; when she looked through glass, everything was tinted with it; when she went to the beach, it was as far as she could see. She hated it because it was inescapable. Blue was too ordinary, too common, and she liked things to be different. She preferred the colour purple.

Anaïs would have painted the sky purple. Which it incidentally was, on occasions. However, occasionally wasn't enough. It had to be all the time. It had to be permanent. Everything blue should be replaced with purple. She would have truckloads of it dumped into the ocean. She would have skywriters spray the heavens with it. She would have blue barred from the planet. She was even willing to live with an excess of green to get it done. And green was her second-most-hated colour. But if she had to make a choice, she would live in a world that was entirely green rather than in this blue-green one.

Her greatest frustration was that she did have the power to change things.

She was a witch.

Anaïs was capable of the most amazing things. She could change people into animals and vice versa. Or, at least, give them the impression it was happening. She could make huge objects disappear. Once she had taken the Empire State Building and put it smack-bang in the middle of London. People had been surprised, until her caretaker had made her put it back and flush the memories of those who had seen it. But the one thing she wanted above all others eluded her. It was an enormous disappointment to her that she didn't have the power to change colour.

Her number one goal was to find the incantation or potion with which to do that. She had tried all the avenues open to her. She had done extensive research and experimented with various concoctions. She had attempted to make contact with those who were more experienced. All to no avail.

She had only found one way to do it. Perception of colour could be changed on an individual basis. So, in order to achieve her goal, she would have to personally cast a spell on every living thing on the planet. Casting the spell was not the problem; that was easy. In fact, it was one of the most basic spells. Even the most inexperienced novice could cast the spell to make someone see something in a different colour. Casting it *en masse* was beyond her capabilities. The best she had achieved was at a Rolling Stones concert. Fifty thousand people was a special achievement. But it was a long way off her ultimate goal. It was also a hollow victory, as most of the audience were already seeing purple anyway.

The problem was that she couldn't do it *physically*. Nor could she make it permanent. She couldn't get rid of one colour and replace it with another. This was especially the case with purple, as it depended entirely on the colour blue for its own existence. So she had shifted her focus to something within her realm of influence. She'd decided to change her surname.

She thought this was doable. It was what had made her dislike the colour blue so excessively in the first place. She really wanted to be Anaïs Purple. She secretly hoped that if she started with her name then perhaps everything else would fall into place.

There was one problem, which she would soon discover: witches have a special relationship with their names. Put simply, it's complicated.

WITCHES

A word of warning: forget everything you think you know about witches. And know this: not all witches are created equal.

I'm no witch but I know enough to consider myself a bit of an expert. If I were one of them, I wouldn't be able to tell you any of this anyway. So, you should consider yourself in a fortunate position. Not everyone has the opportunity to be party to this kind of information. I'll try to keep it short, but we have a lot to cover.

Some of what I have to say will probably seem unimportant or insignificant. I can't be the judge of that. I feel it necessary to impart all I know. I have no idea how long my memory will last and need to pass it on before it gets lost. Maybe you can do something with what I'm about to tell you. At any rate, I feel the pressure of time and don't know how long we will have together.

So let's get started.

Witches provide a connection between the living and the dead. The dead are a notoriously uncommunicative bunch. At the dawn of time it was decided that witches should shoulder the responsibility nobody else wanted. Somebody had to take care of the dead. Straws were drawn and witches ended up with the short one. It's a tough job but someone has to do it.

Some of them are better at it than others. No two witches are alike. Each has their own special skill. Your run-of-the-mill human is no different. We each have our own special gift. The purpose of life is to work out what that is. Unfortunately, some of us never find it. Witches suffer from the same problem. They have one advantage: they know from birth they have a skill. They don't always know what to do with it, but this gives them a head start over the rest of us. Unless they are very lucky, humans only work this out much later in life. Some of us never find our true calling. It's not our fault; it's just the way modern society is structured.

Generally, we humans are brought up to believe that we have to learn something. It doesn't matter what that is. Anything will do. We have to go out and study, or train, or learn a trade. We're driven to do this because we need to get a job. Somewhere in our exponential growth as a modern society, we have forgotten we should be doing what we're good at. Before we even begin we should start by working out what that is. Most of us don't. We just do whatever drops in our lap. We invest huge amounts of time and energy preoccupying ourselves with something we're not suited to. We then either stick it out until the end of our days, or fate steps in and we are forced to change. At which point, we usually try the next best thing that comes along. If we're lucky we chance upon our special skill. If not, we're doomed to a living purgatory until we work out our particular talent. That's another reason we have witches. Someone has to help us find our one, true purpose.

At some point in history the powers that be decided witches were not a good idea. They made witches the enemy and convinced us they were bad. This was incredibly stupid. It complicated an already complex situation. It made no sense to cut the only physical thread between the here and the there. As usual, fear got in the way. Fear of the unknown has caused more misunderstandings, invasions, wars and outright slaughter than anything else. If any power on earth reigns supreme, it is fear. It prevents us from uncovering our special skill.

This is why we need witches. We all need them. Unfortunately, we no longer live in a world which accepts them. We have shot ourselves in our own proverbial feet. It wouldn't be the first time.

Witches are not blessed with a positive image. They are regarded as old and decrepit, feeding on small children. They have a high-pitched cackle and run around turning people into frogs. And then there's the obsession with pointed hats. We are locked into a medieval viewpoint on witches and wizards. This was when the seed for the modern idea of magic was sown. The practitioners in the Middle Ages were generally clergy in apprenticeship, who dabbled in all things spiritual. Their experimentation with summoning demons and such has left us with a warped view of how witchcraft is practised. This has encouraged all kinds of wildly imaginative takes on the subject of necromancy.

The purveyors of fiction have also not been gracious to the witching community. Put simply, the overall view of witches is not good. They are hated, feared and considered evil. From a witch's viewpoint this is disappointing—but also a blessing. It makes for a very good cover-up. To practise any form of supernatural endeavour, you require a certain amount of freedom. Having a good disguise or being able to distract people from reality is advantageous. If you can do this on a large scale without putting in too much effort, even better. Bad press is not necessarily negative. In fact, there's no such thing as bad press. It needs to be manageable but, under certain circumstances, it is preferable.

For the witching population, bad press has been fortuitous. It frees them up for the work they do best without the fear of prying eyes. It is a form of protection.

Before I forget, it might help to take notes. I wish I'd done the same myself when I had the opportunity. Then perhaps I could recall more than I presently do. I have the feeling that just by retelling what I know, the facts will come to light. So please be patient and together we will get to the bottom of this.

Now read carefully and pay attention.

A BABE OUT OF ARMS

Even for a witch, Anaïs Blue was small.

Most witches grow at a more protracted rate than their human counterparts. This is because witches live for a very long time. Living three times the normal human lifespan—or even longer, which is the case with most witches—requires a very slow metabolism. The growth cycle of a witch is more akin to that of a tortoise or a koi. The physical world has its own set of rules, and if you want to live in it you need to abide by these rules. One of the most basic laws of the universe is deterioration. Everything rots. Everything eventually wastes away to nothing. There is no way around this law. Every living thing must abide by it, except perhaps hydra. But nobody really understands them anyway. Apart from them, everything in the physical world will fail the test of time.

Witches are not immortal, they are preternatural. On the outside they age at a barely perceptible rate.

Cognitively, socially, and emotionally they mature at a normal human rate.

Anaïs was a pup on the exterior. She was beyond toilet training, certainly, and all that inconvenient bodily-function stuff. She could feed herself if she wanted to. It wasn't her highest priority and, more often than not, she forgot to eat if she wasn't reminded. Some people enjoy eating. Finding or making the best-tasting food is akin to the search for the holy grail, and every mealtime is a special occasion. Others eat out of necessity. For them, eating is a chore. If there was some other way of pumping energy-enriching vitality into their body without all the preparation and chewing, that would be fantastic. Anaïs belonged to the latter group. She had better things to do with her time than eating.

Putting her disinterest in food aside, Anaïs's biggest problem was her size. Physically she resembled a five-year-old. This was intensely irritating. She just wanted to grow up. Really grow up. Hiding behind her toddler facade was a young woman. She looked five years old, but she was actually seventeen.

The outside world saw someone who had just learnt the basics. They saw a small child who could walk and talk and do little else of great importance. She had the same problem as most five-year-olds: nobody takes them seriously. Small children usually do themselves a disservice. Nobody wants to hear incessant chatter about how you just discovered the difference between a feather and leaf. There is also an irritating preoccupation with sticks, water and sand.

Anaïs was beyond all this. Sticks and such were no

longer playthings. She was more than capable of holding a lucid conversation, which she invariably did with anyone who cared to listen. But nobody expected her to say anything of value. People rarely heard her opinions on world affairs or her comments on the strength of the American dollar. They switched off the moment she opened her mouth.

This was not without its benefits. Living in the body of a five-year-old had a lot of positives. In some ways it was the perfect disguise if you knew how to use your status in the world. As a witch it was an especially favourable position. For Anaïs, it was the most advantageous time of her life.

As adults tend to ignore strange behaviour in young children, she could do practically whatever she wanted. Grown-ups don't pay close attention to what a child is doing. Generally, if a child is happily occupied it will be left alone. If a child is accompanied by an adult, it will be completely ignored. Adults are willing to let children do anything as long as they know it has been okayed by a parent or guardian.

This was an essential requirement for Anaïs to be able to roam freely as a witch. Even though she could be left to her own devices, whenever she went out in public she needed to be chaperoned by an adult. It also didn't hurt that an adult was useful for reminding her to eat. For these purposes, Anaïs had Nan.

THE NANNY

naïs carried around an entire file system of notes stuffed in her pockets. If you're a small child, a letter from your mother can get you places. If you are able to compose those letters yourself, so much the better. Then you have total control. What you are able to do would only be limited by your imagination. Anaïs didn't have a mother to write her notes. Instead, she had Nan. And even though Anaïs had her notes, Nan rarely let her go out on her own.

Her nanny, or Nan for short, was in her early thirties. She was tall and slender and quite beautiful, but had a coarse edge. She was strict and not someone to be crossed. She was not what you would expect from a nursemaid. Nan had been with Anaïs since she had been separated from her mother when she was six years of age. At this time Anaïs had begun to display the first traits of a witch. The Organisation had elicited the help of Nan and sent Anaïs to live with her.

It has been said that with great power comes great

responsibility. This is especially true in the case of witches. It is generally accepted that women rule the earth. They are the mothers, and not only in a biological sense. They are the caretakers of the planet. In some cultures the earth itself is considered a mother. Women make sure men don't stuff it all up.

In order to take care of the planet there has to be some form of quality control. There has to be a structure or formal skeleton to work from. Everyone can't just run riot and do what they please. Hoping for the best won't work. Some form of management is required. There needs to be an organisation.

As with many planet-wide administrative bodies The World Witch Organisation grew organically out of need. In the beginning the world had no global unity. Each country or region was self-managed. Some were more successful than others. Some were complete disasters. There were wars and such with immediate neighbours. They were like little islands fighting to maintain their individual independence and way of life. In more recent times this has all changed and the islands have been bridged. There is now much more freedom of movement and interaction. This presents its own set of problems. Sometimes it's necessary to have something or someone to supervise it all. Freedom has a price. In order for it to survive it needs to be managed.

The history of the world for witches has been no different. Like the rest of the peoples of the world, it took some time for individual witches on the planet to realise they weren't alone. This primarily revealed itself through inclement weather. Too much psychic power gathered in one place is unmanageable and has a tendency to be destructive. We won't go into specifics. Needless to say, witches realised they weren't alone. Over time their numbers grew and it became necessary to manage their affairs and bring in some form of committee as overseer. The World Witch Organisation grew out of this necessity.

Nan was one of the few naturals, or normal humans, who was party to this inner circle of witches. This honour was not bestowed on just anyone. You needed a specific skill-set. Nan had this. She knew what made a witch tick. She was the daughter of one. She could relate to Anaïs through her own experiences. Not that she was forced to be apart from her mother. That had been a personal choice. Not all families live in a constant harmonious state. Kin that don't have disagreements are as rare as witches giving birth to other witches. Nan and her mother couldn't stand one another. But apart from her own mother, Nan liked being around witches. She wished she had been born as one. She needed a substitute. She found one in Anaïs.

It wasn't an easy relationship. Quite often Anaïs thought Nan was a pain in the butt. She grappled with the usual things a child has to deal with when under the supervision of someone older and perhaps wiser:

Who is this person?

What right has she to order me around?

She isn't the boss of me.

I know what I'm doing.

Stop telling me what to do.

You aren't my mother.

Leave me alone.

Perfectly normal reactions. As Anaïs aged she struggled more and more with the restrictions of her physical self. Her mental self wanted freedom. It wanted to roam. It was sick of being stuck in the same place. It yearned to see the world. It didn't want to be mothered. It wanted to be treated like the growing adult that it was. It couldn't be, though. The five-year-old body she was wrapped in needed help. It couldn't do it alone.

Nan liked her role but could see in her relationship with Anaïs a reflection of the rebelliousness she had expressed towards her own mother, and knew it was going to create problems. She didn't want to lose Anaïs in the way her own mother had lost her. She didn't want to ostracise Anaïs or become the enemy. She wanted to be friends. But being a friend and a parent is a difficult balance to maintain, like precariously wandering across thin ice. Nan couldn't truly be either one. She was more like the hired help. Twelve years was a long time to be with someone you weren't related to. She felt morally responsible; then again, if she really wanted to, she could walk away. She had begun to think what it would be like to have a life of her own. She wondered if she still had it in her to find someone for herself, or if she was even capable of having a meaningful relationship out in the real world.

Both women were in the same situation. They were beginning to rub each other the wrong way. Anger was brewing. Nan had to curb her own desires. She had to reduce the friction between them or it might get out of control. She didn't know what an angry witch was capable of. Maybe it was something to be feared. She had thought to consult The Organisation about these developments but decided to attempt to solve it herself, at least for the time being. After all, she knew Anaïs better than anyone else. And so, she had formulated a plan to allow for some more time apart. It would be better for them both if Anaïs was let out on a longer leash. Possibly Anaïs could find some new friends. She needed to do something useful and she should develop her skills. Nan couldn't really help her in that department. Although Nan despised the thought, she knew the time had come. Anaïs should do more things on her own.

Anaïs wasn't particularly lonely. She had Nan to talk to. But one person wasn't enough to fill her world. It would be better to have different people to bounce stuff off. She regretted there wasn't anyone her own age to hang out with. But therein lay the problem. There were physical barriers to her making friends. If you're only a metre tall and look as though you have just graduated from nappies, then you are not going to attract the sort of attention you want. A bunch of adults cooing over you and calling you cute doesn't cut it in the teen stakes either. There's no honour in that. It's uncool. Apart from the change of name, Anaïs simply wanted to grow up.

She had spent too many years trapped in her petite prison. It was getting on her nerves.

GROUNDED

Anaïs stared at her hands.

Damn these baby hands, she thought.

She twiddled her thumbs. She dropped her shoulders and sulked. It was the fourth time this week that Nan had sent her to her room. She was getting too old for this kind of thing. She wasn't a baby anymore. Couldn't Nan see that? Anaïs looked down at her body and regrettably answered her own question. No, Nan couldn't see that. Nan only saw a small child, a five-year-old.

She looked around her room. It was filled with everything a little girl could want: dolls and stuffed toys, make-up and plastic jewellery, Lego. She even had a four-poster canopy bed. Everything was gaudily coloured; everything sparkled. Once, she had been obsessed by little brightly-coloured plastic things. She would spend hours studying their tiny details. Everything had to be vividly coloured. Everything had to twinkle or flash bright lights. She had been like a crow. This wasn't her anymore. It hadn't been her for a long time. She wasn't a little girl; she was practically an adult. She was going to be eighteen in a few days. Why didn't Nan remember this?

She was sick of carrying on the charade of being a helpless toddler. Sure, she was limited physically, and it was necessary to maintain that performance in public. But in private it should be different. They weren't that far apart in age. Nan could only be ten or fifteen years older.

Why is Nan in charge anyway? I can take care of myself. I don't need any help.

She flipped through the pages of her promptuary. Maybe there was a spell she could cast. Maybe there was a concoction she could drop in Nan's drink so that she could give her the slip. She wanted out. She wanted to be alone. She didn't want this overbearing adult dictating her life anymore. She'd had enough of being ordered around. She would tell Nan what she thought of her. She became worked up. She grabbed a Barbie doll and tried unsuccessfully to twist off its leg. She didn't have the strength. That frustrated her even more. She threw the doll into the far corner of her bedroom. It bounced off the pink blow-up teddy bear and flew back towards her. She ducked to avoid it.

She looked down at the promptuary. The open page lit up. It showed her Nan sitting alone in the kitchen. She looked unhappy. She was staring vacantly into the empty coffee cup in her hands. Anaïs watched as Nan squeezed the cup tightly. The whites of her knuckles showed and the cup handle snapped off under the pressure. Nan sighed, her shoulders lifting and dropping. She released her grip on the cup, picked up the broken handle and threw it towards the bin in the corner. It shattered against the wall.

Anaïs looked up from the book when she heard the sound through her bedroom door. It was pointless getting angry with Nan. It was also unfair. Nan was in the same position. Nan was trapped, just like her.

For the first time, she thought for a moment what it must be like for Nan. She hadn't considered Nan's predicament before. It was a new way of thinking for her.

Where did this thought come from? Is this what growing up is all about?

She was confused. Maybe they just needed to talk about it. Usually Nan settled the arguments. Anaïs thought about it for a minute. She also had control over the situation. They didn't need to fight. She could make peace. If she did then maybe Nan would look at her differently. Maybe Nan would see the adult in her and treat her more as an equal.

It was worth a try. She dropped the idea of working with spells. She didn't need one to manipulate the situation. She could communicate like a natural. They did it all the time, so why couldn't she? It would certainly have a longer-lasting effect. Spells wore off. They had a use-by-date. Real emotions were more effective. She would broach the subject. She would make the first move. They were sort-of family, but not really. It was healthier if she treated Nan as an equal. It was better if she and Nan became friends. Besides, anger cost her an enormous amount of energy, and eventually led to nought. She would be better off putting her energy into something more useful.

She put the promptuary down, picked up the doll and placed it on her bedside table. Its leg was contorted at a peculiar angle. She twisted the limb back into position.

If only relationships could be repaired as easily as plastic toys.

She smoothed down the front of her dress, made a similar mental adjustment, cracked open her bedroom door and walked down the corridor with the air of someone much older than she looked.

THE WITCHES HANDBOOK

T he witch's handbook, or promptuary as it is
officially known, is one of the most important
objects in a witch's arsenal. All witches have
their own copy.

Handbooks vary in size but most of them resemble a
pocket dictionary. In ancient times, before the advent of
paper, witches were forced to carry more cumbersome
versions of the handbook around, usually in the form of
bamboo scrolls.

Herein lies a major fallacy concerning witches.
There is a misconception that witches have magic
wands. Perceptions of witches are rarely correct. Over
the centuries the depiction of a witch and her scroll
changed. At some point the image of a scroll was
whittled down to a stick. A stick has no power. A witch's
handbook does. It holds immense knowledge, and
knowledge is power. As a witch grows and develops she
discovers more about her special traits. All this
knowledge is recorded in the handbook.

Incidentally, if it hadn't been for witches, paper wouldn't have been invented as early as it was. In particular the use of paper to write things down on. If it hadn't been for witches we would still be using it to wipe our posteriors, wrap up our groceries and pack valuable objects.

The Chinese were the first to be blessed with the recipe for paper. One particularly inventive witch in the Gansu Province had been experimenting with making something to wrap her potions in. She hit upon the idea for paper one day whilst trying to pound a rag wafer-thin. In no time, the discovery spread swiftly through the witch community. Eventually, the Chinese arm of The Organisation decided to reveal the knowledge to humanity, in order to precipitate development of the material. The rest is history.

This was one of the rare occasions when a decision was made to assist naturals in their advancement. Normally this would not happen. Witches are not permitted to do anything that permanently influences the human race. It was a question of practicality. They got sick of carrying around bamboo scrolls.

Because witches cannot congregate, the promptuary provides one of the few avenues of communication between them. Aside from functioning as a messaging service, promptuaries also do more mundane things, such as providing news and maps. They are capable of more than can be imagined. No witch has ever fully utilised its potential.

The main differences between a handbook and a modern mobile device is the power supply and the material from which it is constructed. Electronics are not infallible, and witches would never rely on something so sensitive or prone to breaking down. Over time witches have developed paper and imbued it with extraordinary properties. Although promptuaries outwardly suffer from heavy usage, they are virtually indestructible. They have become an entity unto themselves. A promptuary has to last a lifetime, and for a witch that is exceedingly long.

Just like a name, a promptuary is specific to an individual. It will react upon the core desires of its owner. It can be commanded to do specific things, but this requires extensive experience. It's of no use to someone who has not made the same journey through life. There are no advantages to possessing someone else's promptuary. You need to gain the knowledge before it goes into the book. You cannot properly understand something without having experienced it first-hand. It is counterproductive. As in all realms of the universe, only honestly acquired knowledge is useful.

Spurious knowledge is worthless.

A NEW NAME

As she walked down the corridor Anaïs stuck her hands in her pockets. It was there. Anaïs sighed.

She couldn't recall where or when she had first received her promptuary. It had always been there. It never left her side. She had experimented with hiding it in obscure places. She had piled heavy objects on it and left the house. She had even purposely left it behind in restaurants and museums. She had done everything in her power to lose it. It made no difference. It always found its way back. It would deposit itself in her pocket, or she would move something on a table and it would suddenly appear. She never felt it. It weighed nothing. It was only when she held it in her hand that she sensed the weight of its knowledge. As its contents grew, so did its mass.

Sometimes Anaïs hated her promptuary. She knew how important it was but she rarely used it. It was an irritation and she often treated it with contempt. The promptuary suffered from lack of attention. It was dog-eared like an old school book. If she continued to treat it this way, within a century or two it would be reduced to a tattered mess.

Recently, she had come to accept that it was a constant in her life. She was resigned to the fact that it would never leave her. There was something reassuring about that. Whatever happened, she could trust it to be by her side. It wasn't exactly a friend, but in some way it was a soul mate. Apart from Nan, the promptuary was the one constant in her life.

Anaïs pulled it out and turned it over in her hand. She ran her fingers over its contours and across the big, smooth star on its cover. The star reacted to her touch and lit up. She opened the book. Printed in glowing block letters on the page was one word: *shade*.

Anaïs hadn't thought about it before, but a shade might be the solution. Finding a shade to hang out with might solve her problem. At least on the face of it, Anaïs could walk the streets without being chaperoned by her caretaker.

Nan had taken some time to come to terms with this. She knew Anaïs would be able to take care of herself. It was mainly a question of trust. She forgot that she wasn't dealing with a toddler sometimes.

Anaïs shut the book and continued down the corridor and into the kitchen. Nan brightened when she saw her.

'Hey, Blue.'

Nan rarely called Anaïs by her first name. It was too formal.

Anaïs screwed up her face. 'Don't call me that.'

'What?'

'Blue.'

'Oh? Really? What should I call you then?'

'Purple.'

'Mmm, I don't know about that. I like Blue.'

Anaïs frowned. 'No, it's my name, my choice. I don't like blue. Blue sucks. I want to be called Purple.'

'Fine, but I don't feel like calling out "Purple" all the time. Maybe I could just use your first name?'

'No, when you do that it feels like you're telling me off. I prefer a colour.'

Nan sighed. There was no point in arguing. It was clear, at least for the moment, that Anaïs was fixed in her desire. Nan was used to her flightiness. One minute she would be obsessed with something, and the next it would be completely forgotten. It would be best just to humour her for the moment. She would probably change her mind later.

'Ok, then maybe we need to look for alternatives. Aren't there different shades of purple?'

Anaïs thought for moment and then opened her promptuary. She spoke into it. 'What are the different shades of purple?'

The book glowed and began speaking. 'Tyrian Purple, Han Purple, Royal Purple, Mauveine, Thistle, Orchid.'

Anaïs's eyes widened. 'Stop! That's it.'

Nan looked first at her and then at the book. 'Which one? Orchid?'

Anaïs shook her head. 'No, not Orchid, Thistle. Thistle, that's cool. Call me that. Call me Thistle.'

'Hmm, maybe. It's better than Purple.'

'C'mon, Nan, please.'

Nan looked at her pleading face. For a moment she forgot that behind the earnest green eyes was a young woman and not a child. The eyes got her every time. She conceded. 'Ok, but it's going to take a bit of getting used to.'

Anaïs did a jig on the spot. 'Fantastic. Go on, try it.'

Nan rolled her eyes and stared at the ceiling. She cleared her throat. 'How are you today, Thistle?'

'No, you wouldn't talk to me like that. Do it properly.'

'Ok.'

Nan took a deep breath. She composed herself and looked Anaïs straight in the eye. 'Hey, Thistle, shall we go shopping?'

The lights in the house dipped and came back on. It was the middle of the day and they barely noticed it.

Anaïs grinned. 'Cool. Are you serious?'

'What?'

'About going shopping.'

Nan realised she should still be punishing Anaïs but saw a way to reconnect. 'Sure. Let's go shopping.'

Anaïs beamed. 'Great.'

'There's just one thing.'

The little witch frowned. 'What?'

Nan indicated the pieces of shattered crockery strewn across the floor. 'Have you forgotten what you did?'

'Oh. Yeah, I'm sorry. I lost it.'

'It's fine. I lost it too. I shouldn't have yelled at you like that. Friends?'

Anaïs smiled at her. 'Yeah, friends.'

Nan pushed her chair back and stood up. 'Ok. We'll clean this up when we get back. Let's go then.'

Anaïs did her little-girl jig again. 'Yes, let's go. We haven't shopped for ages!'

COOKING UP A SPELL

Most people assume that spells and incantations are mysterious things. They are under the misconception that they float about in the air. They think that with the utterance of a few choice words, everything is launched into action. This is not so.

In order for a spell to work it must be attached to something physical, preferably an inanimate object. If you were to speak a few magic words and release them into the world they would just dissipate into thin air, or float off on the wind. There is a slim chance that they would collide with their intended target, but the probability of that is low. If witches were to operate in such a fashion, the world would be in chaos. You can't just throw around your power like that. It's dangerous. It would be like a continuous sequence of hit-and-runs. Nobody would have any idea what the hell was going on. It might bring about the end of life on earth as we know it.

When it comes to casting spells on naturals, food has proved to be the best form of conveyance. Anaïs had her favourites. In most circumstances the following substances worked on her subjects: lollies for children, chocolate for women and beer for men. Once her spell was ingested with these products, she was almost always guaranteed success. Planting spells in food also makes it easier to get past the world's most advanced security system—the human body.

The active participation of the receiver is required for an incantation to function properly. Spells only work if there is pinpoint accuracy. They need to fit their receivers. If they don't they will be rejected. The human body is designed to protect itself. It will not allow a foreign body of any description to enter it uninvited. It ensures this on several levels, the molecular, the sub-atomic, the mental and the physical. There is also the paranormal. The human body is a mass of sensors. It's like one of those irritating car alarms that goes off the moment you breathe in its vicinity. But the sensitivity of the human body is multiplied by a factor of millions. Nothing escapes its attention. If you wish to introduce a foreign object into a body, you have to be devious. You need to perform more than one trick in order to perform the trick that you are trying to perform. If you don't have your wits about you it can get very confusing.

Casting a spell requires a great deal of preparation and an intimate knowledge of cooking. Not all witches are good cooks. That is why take-away spells were conceived. It's also the natural order of things. The human race has become more efficient as time has progressed. This has not only had an effect on how food is produced but also the kinds of food there are. If you went back to America during the Civil War you wouldn't find people going out for pizza. If you were to offer dim sum to a Roman centurion, they probably would think you were trying to poison them.

Anaïs could boil water and that was about it. This was not necessarily a major problem. You can achieve a lot just by boiling water. You can cook an egg, brew a cup of tea, or prepare a bowl of rice. Dehydrated food has come a long way and, if you desire, you can prepare just about anything by adding water. So essentially all a witch has to do is cast a spell into water and add something flavoursome to it. Then they try to get their target to eat or drink whatever they have prepared. The more appetising the concoction the better. Nobody is willingly going to consume a bowl of cold rice. You need to be inventive. Therefore, cooking classes are central to all advanced witch training.

The variety and types of cuisine, once limited to particular regions, has spread exponentially across the globe. Much of this is a result of the experimentation of witches. A disproportionate number of witches are chefs. In fact, most of the female Michelin Star chefs on the planet are witches. And, as most of the male Michelin Star chefs are tasting their food, they are invariably under the effect of spells. This in turn has led to a proliferation of cooking programs on television.

At some stage The Organisation became aware that this was getting out of hand. The more exposure there was to proficient cooking in which witches were involved, the more danger there was of revealing who was behind it all. Keeping a low profile remains the highest priority for most of the community. Occasionally one or two witches would get carried away by the lure of cooking fame. Then a representative from The Organisation would step in and put an end to their career. It was nothing personal, merely a necessary requirement. Witches had to be reminded that cooking was purely a means to an end.

For the most part, witches were content to use the dehydrated form of a spell. It was more practical and much less time-consuming than making it yourself. Unless you were considering something out of the ordinary. Something like getting people to see the colour blue as purple. Then special skills were required. Fortunately, Anaïs's place of residence meant she was in contact with the best in the business.

An underground trade in spells had grown out of the need for these specific concoctions. The ancient art of the apothecary still flourished. Amsterdam has a long history of trade, and at one time had been the centre of the world for exotic goods. This centralisation has persisted, and Amsterdam is blessed with one of the best-stocked apothecaries in the world. For those in the know, the Apotheek was the go-to place for all their special requirements.

THE APOTHEEK

The Apotheek was well hidden. There was no such thing as an official entrance. There were in fact several entrances, but Nan and Anaïs only knew of one. It was behind a concealed door in a changing room at the rear of a dress shop. Anaïs was one of the few who regularly visited the shop in person.

The word 'shop' didn't really adequately describe the Apotheek. It was more of a storehouse. In modern times, and since the explosion of online shopping—also something which had been subtly influenced by witches —it was no longer necessary to visit an apothecary in person. Amsterdam is centrally placed in Europe and had become one of the major sources of witch paraphernalia. The Apotheek was well known in the community and shipped its wares to all corners of the globe.

Throughout history apothecaries have not catered exclusively to witches, but in recent times certain members of this guild had turned to specialising in providing various under-the-counter concoctions. The trade of mind-enhancing drugs becoming illegal had driven members of the guild underground. Many had previously worked for the military and had gleaned most of their knowledge from their time in the service.

Anaïs had been given special access to the Apotheek by The Organisation. The code to open the entrance had been loaded into her promptuary. Nan and Anaïs stood inside the changing room and Anaïs waved her book in front of a seemingly innocent wall. It slid to one side and they stepped into a small, square alcove. The wall to the changing room slid shut. A single bare light bulb hung on exposed wires above their heads, barely illuminating what was now a dark box. There was a clunk and the floor beneath their feet shook and began to descend. After a few moments the movement stopped and another wall slid aside. They squinted as stark, bright light flooded in. They stepped out into it.

Anaïs loved the shop. Everything gleamed. The store looked as if high-gloss white plastic had been sprayed on everything. The covering was so complete that the walls could barely be seen to meet the floor. The walls themselves were covered in a uniform grid of thin, black horizontal and vertical lines. Hundreds of little drawers. At the centre of each drawer was a small pinpoint of light. Most glowed faintly, but others winked on and off.

The room was open and spacious. There was very little on display except for a solitary glass cabinet in the middle. The cabinet was filled with a collection of ancient implements and tools. Several narrow corridors branched off the room. They seemed to stretch on forever. From the end of one of these corridors footsteps approached. With them came the increasing sound of white noise.

The apothecary rarely had visitors. He was in his late twenties and, apart from a white smock, didn't look at all like a pharmacologist. Under the smock he wore a pair of baggy sports pants. On his feet were boat-sized basketball sneakers with loose laces which tapped the floor as he walked. He sported a baseball cap pulled down low over his face so that his eyes could barely be seen. An oversized set of headphones bridged his skull. They were the source of the white noise.

The apothecary swaggered out of the corridor. He nearly tripped over his laces and stopped to untangle them before crossing the room. 'Hey, Anaïs, how's it hanging?' he said cheerfully.

He held out his fist. She made a fist herself and tapped his knuckles with her own.

She smiled up at him. 'Excellent!'

'Listen to this.' He pulled off his headphones. The shrill sound of distorted guitar filled the room. He yelled above the din, 'Just rediscovered this little gem. It's an oldie but it rocks.'

He bent down and wrapped the headphones around her head. Anaïs cupped both hands around the earpieces and nodded her head to the music.

She looked up at him and yelled, 'What's it called?'

He pulled one of the earpieces away from her head and yelled back, 'White Punks on Dope!'

The apothecary nestled the earpiece back into position and looked at Nan. 'How are things, sister?'

Nan shrugged and stared at the ceiling. She didn't like the place. She nudged Anaïs, who pulled the headphones off. The music filled the room again. The apothecary searched his pockets and pulled out a mobile phone. He squinted at it and tapped its screen. The music died. The sound lingered for a moment, reverberating down the corridors and back at them.

'C'mon, let's get what you want and go,' said Nan.

Anaïs raised her eyebrows at the apothecary. 'Ok, ok.'

He took the headphones from Anaïs and sneered at Nan.

'Did you get my mail?' Anaïs inquired.

'Yep, sure. Give me a minute.' He walked to the nearest wall and held his phone against one of the drawers. It slid open with a swishing sound. He reached in and pulled out a small silver box. He gave it to Anaïs. 'Remember, no more than one every four hours. It's pretty powerful stuff.'

'Thanks, I'll remember that.'

'Good, you'd better.' He winked at her. 'Otherwise they might not snap out of it.'

'What is it?' asked Nan.

'Just one of our little experiments,' said Anaïs, and threw a private smile at the apothecary.

Anaïs removed her purple beret and dropped the silver box into it. The hat swallowed it up. She reached in and rummaged around inside. Her arm went in up to her elbow but the beret maintained its shape. It looked as if her arm had been cut off at the elbow and she was holding the stump in the palm of her hand with the hat.

'I've really got to get myself one of those,' said the apothecary.

'Sorry,' said Anaïs. 'Can't help you there. One of the perks of the job.' She winked at him and there was genuine disappointment on his face. She withdrew her arm and handed him a crisp hundred-euro note.

'Thanks. Pleasure doing business with you. I would prefer the beret, though.'

Anaïs smiled at him and turned to Nan. 'It's ok, we can go now.'

'Don't be a stranger,' said the apothecary. 'Maybe next time we can listen to more of that old stuff. I've got a cool sound system set up out back.' He waved his arm down one of the corridors.

'Yeah, that'd be great.' Anaïs shot a questioning look at Nan.

Nan was noncommittal and murmured through her teeth, 'Maybe.'

Anaïs pursed her lips. 'I guess that's better than a straight-out *no*.'

'No worries, it's cool. I'll mail you something to wrap your ears around,' said the apothecary.

'Nice,' said Anaïs.

'See you next time,' he said to Nan.

She ignored him and led the way back to the alcove. 'Right, let's do some real shopping.'

Anaïs followed reluctantly. 'Ciao,' she said over shoulder to the apothecary.

'Ciao,' he said and tapped his phone. The room filled with noise and then dulled dramatically when he clamped the headphones back over his ears.

HATS AND BERETS

Fashion dictates what is in, and what is out. The wearing of hats is no exception. It was once common for people to don headwear. A man wouldn't be seen dead without his hat. There was a whole wash-list of etiquette attached to them. Not wearing them inside was one such protocol, as was tipping them as a sign of courtesy.

A witch doesn't need a hat. Some prefer to travel light. There are negative sides to having a hat. Keeping up with fashion is just one of them. Witches are not limited to a particular style, either. The pointy hat, traditionally associated with witches, is great for keeping the rain off your head but not much more. Although it's incredibly spacious, which can be advantageous, it's also cumbersome. There are, of course, those who swear by them. The style of the headgear itself is a question of personal preference. What they can perform is far more important.

A witch's hat can provide all kinds of protection, and

not just against precipitation. It can prevent others from reading your thoughts. It can even deflect lightning and other electrical activity. If used properly it can convert into a full-length disguise.

Anaïs swore by her hat. She never went anywhere without it. It took the form of a beret and was, naturally, purple. She used it predominantly for storage. Every now and then it got so full she had to clean it out. It was symbolic that it sat on her head. It was her portable attic and, like most attics, it was full of junk.

Living in a big city has advantages. As a witch you need to keep your identity secret, the most obvious reason being that you age incredibly slowly. In a country town everybody knows everybody and, unfortunately, gingerbread houses attract lots of attention. Cities are good places to keep a low profile. They also allow freedom of movement. If you are exposed you don't have to move to an entirely different place; you can just move to the next suburb.

People are always moving around in cities. If your neighbour moves, you can easily lose contact with them, even though they may only move a few streets away. It's even possible to remain incognito with people in your own apartment block. As long as you keep your head down nobody will notice you. You will blend in. Sometimes the best place to hide is within a crowd.

There were plenty of places to hide in Amsterdam. No matter how long you lived there you would never exhaust all of its nooks and crannies. Anaïs and Nan had moved several times, and both had played a hand in being required to move house. Not only the occasional magical slip-up by Anaïs, but Nan's rough character tended to upset neighbours.

The beret had become her mobile wardrobe. It was handy. If they had to move in a hurry, they could. Everything of importance was in her beret. She dreaded the day when it would go out of fashion and she would be forced to find another form of headwear. Then she would have to do a major spring clean. As it was, she was having difficulty finding things.

With her hat and her promptuary, she felt like a walking removal van at times. Like a turtle lugging her shell around. This was one part of her life as a witch she wished could be different. The constant threat of being discovered, and having to find a new dwelling, gave her a feeling of homelessness.

SHOPPING

Anaïs walked out of the changing room. 'What do you think?'

She wore a pair of black jeans and a pale purple t-shirt. There were no sparkles or imprints of hearts. The edges of the shirt weren't even frilled. In her somewhat more mature clothing, she looked so much older.

'Wow! What happened to my baby?' Nan exclaimed and clapped her hands to her face in mock shock.

Anaïs giggled. 'She's in the dressing room.'

'Oh.' Nan's face dropped.

She was genuinely disappointed. Nan could see that, small stature or not, Anaïs was in the process of breaking out. Nothing could prevent this. It was just a natural progression. Even witches grow up. It reminded her of her own teen years. She had rebelled, totally and unequivocally. But then she and her mother had the added complication of a vast difference in age. Her mother was at least three hundred years old. Not that she wasn't cool. Considering her age, she was definitely hip. But she was career motivated, and having a daughter was more of an anchor than an asset. She had taken on a great deal of responsibility, and being a mother was a minor consideration. She had more important obligations. She was one of the longest-standing members of The World Witch Organisation.

Anaïs noted Nan's dismay. 'Oh come on, Nan, don't be like that. I'm still here, at least for the moment.'

'That's what bothers me. How long will the moment last?'

Anaïs furrowed her brow and looked sternly up at Nan. 'If it was up to me it would be for a very long time. I'm not like your mother.'

Nan's mood lightened, but there was an emotional edge to her voice. It broke as she spoke. 'Good, glad to hear it.' She cleared her throat. 'And please don't mention that woman. Now go and get changed.'

Anaïs looked down at her new clothes and folded her arms across her chest. 'No, I don't want to. Can't I keep these on?'

Nan looked her up and down and sighed. 'I suppose so, but you'll need some new shoes.'

'Cool! I'll be right back.'

Anaïs ran into the dressing room, leaving Nan with lingering thoughts of her mother. Her mother's neglect, out of duty to her position, meant they had fought like cats. The damage to their relationship had been so complete that they now refused to talk to one another. When they did communicate, it was always through an intermediary.

Nan didn't want things to go the same way with her and Anaïs. She had tried to make up for her own feelings of abandonment. She had pampered Anaïs and gone out of her way to give her everything she felt she'd missed. She had made Anaïs her number one priority. It now saddened her to see that some of her responsibilities were eroding. Anaïs's powers had developed markedly and the time was fast approaching when she would be able to fend for herself. It dawned on Nan that very soon even the petite body would not provide an obstacle.

Anaïs came out of the dressing room. 'I'm hungry. Can we get the shoes a bit later?'

Nan considered her request for a moment. 'Sure.'

'Can I have some money?'

Nan gave her a disapproving look. 'Why?'

Anaïs puffed her cheeks in frustration. 'So I can get something to eat.'

She really was growing up. 'And what about me?'

'I want to do it alone. You don't like chicken burgers, anyway.'

Nan was wary of putting too many restrictions on her. It was time to give her a bit more freedom, and now was as good a moment as any.

'Fair enough, go get yourself a burger.' She handed Anaïs some money. 'But don't be too long. I'll wait for you in the cafe next door.'

Anaïs was pleased. She hadn't thought Nan would relent so easily. 'Ok.' She eagerly took the money. 'See you soon.'

'Wait a minute.'

'What?' It was too good to be true. Nan wasn't really going to let her go.

Nan pointed at the white cardboard square hanging from her sleeve. 'I need the price tags.'

Anaïs coloured with embarrassment. 'Oh, yeah, you're right.'

Together they removed the tags. Nan gave her a kiss and watched her skip her way to the shop's entrance. She had the overwhelming urge to follow but forced herself to stay put. She had to trust Anaïs.

Once Anaïs had left the shop, Nan went to the cash register and paid for the clothes. However, as soon as she had completed the transaction, her plan changed. She didn't feel comfortable leaving Anaïs alone. Once outside, she went directly to the burger shop in search of her.

THE DEAD

Have you ever had your eye caught by someone in a crowd? Maybe you spotted someone across a room or on a bus. Maybe you thought nothing of it but when you looked back they were gone. Be assured you weren't imagining things; you've been shaded.

The dead walk among us. It's something we're not always aware of. Generally, they keep to themselves and don't communicate with the living. Surprisingly, they do travel in human form. The dead should not be confused with zombies; they are in no way associated. Zombies are a fabrication, and the idea stems from an unfortunate period when the dead were noticed by the general public.

After the Black Death, the deceased population expanded exponentially and began taking liberties with their appearance. Steps were taken to force them to blend in. They are certainly now more aware of their standing in the world and have realised it is fortuitous to keep their existence concealed. However, for the good of all concerned, a number of barriers were put in place to prevent communication. Otherwise it would be a free-for-all.

Witches are among the few entities who are aware of the dead. They can spot them a mile away. Beings of a lifeless persuasion are actually quite easy to identify. The dead don't have shadows.

The living are not generally observant enough to spot this deficiency. They are too busy doing other things. The modern world, with all its hustle and bustle and people's obsession with stress, has been kind to the dead. If more people were to take time out from their busy lives and take the effort to look at the ground beneath them, they would be surprised.

The dead are more active in winter, when there's less sun. They are rarely out and about at dusk or dawn, when shadows are at their longest. Now that you are aware of this, it should come as no surprise that there are always many more people around in any large city at lunchtime. The population in any one part of the planet doubles between the hours of noon and two o'clock in the afternoon. Have you never wondered why? Due to the virtual non-existence of shadows, the dead are especially fond of midday.

However, night-time is naturally the best time for the dead. Shadows are everywhere. For the dead, darkness is like a warm blanket. The night is wonderful. It's possible to get away with so much more in the dark. Without light, the world is transformed. Everything looks different, and certain objects even improve aesthetically.

Some of the ugliest buildings look their best in the dark. This also goes for certain people. There is beauty in darkness. The dead love the night. It's their favourite time to play. They have a freedom of movement that doesn't exist in the daytime.

You might wonder why the dead, if they are in plain sight, don't stand out. You might assume some of them would be walking around in sixteenth-century ballgowns with fifty petticoats underneath. The dead are, after all, laid to rest in something. Not many are buried naked. If the dead paraded around in their burial attire, the world would be filled with an inordinate number of military personnel in various forms of battle dress.

The dead are bestowed with a cloaking device. Under their disguises they are, indeed, wearing their funeral attire; but over that is a sort of sheen, a form of camouflage, which adapts to its surroundings. Say one of them were to walk into a bar. Then their camouflage would automatically clothe them in jeans and a t-shirt. In the business sector at rush hour they would be decked out in suits and ties. Their real clothing is not the only thing that is hidden. The same goes for their physical appearance. As with their clothing, their faces and physical characteristics are not revealed to the living. Of course, they are not rotting, with maggots and stuff coming out of their ears. That wouldn't make sense. Behind the facade they are frozen in time.

It is possible to see their underlying attributes, but only in a mirror. It's practically a vampire thing—not that they exist. But whereas a vampire is traditionally invisible in a mirror, it works opposite for the dead.

Mirrors strip the deceased of all their camouflage. You see them for who they really are. If you stand in front of a mirror you are, after all, wanting to check out your appearance, whatever that may be. Mirrors never lie; they always show the real you.

This creates another problem for the dead. Avoiding reflective surfaces and mirrors can be difficult. There is glass everywhere and sunlight, even when veiled behind cloud, shines the whole day through. If you're dead, it's not advisable to parade in front of windows.

All these things—the lack of shadow; the reflections; the disguise and camouflage—have led to witches adopting a special name for the dead. The word 'dead' is particularly derogatory and not acceptable in this modern age.

Witches call the dead 'shades'.

Shades are doomed to a world of insomnia. The whole idea of eternal rest is a fallacy. It is more like eternal unrest. Once you leave the supposed world of the living, you have to suffer an eternity of sleeplessness. The dead have very little to do, and naturally have to go somewhere. They are just like you and me and crave human companionship. For most of the day they are in hiding or trying to maintain a low profile. But, when given the opportunity, they still prefer to be part of a crowd.

Witches and shades have the same relationships we all have. With some people we click, with others, not. Some people can help us; some can be confidants; some can be lovers. It is reciprocal. Not everyone can fill our specific holes. It's a question of searching and making contact with as many people as possible. Eventually you will find your match. For shades, this is all the more complicated. They don't know who they can communicate with. Only a witch has the ability to spot them. The auto-camouflage prevents shades from reaching out to everyone.

Shades have very little to do and spend most of their time just hanging around. It's a frustrating existence. There is no sense of achievement. Time goes by incredibly slowly if you have nothing to do. It helps having someone to share your existence with.

Unsurprisingly, the main drive for a drifting soul is to find a new entity to reside in. Then at least they can get some rest. If you never get to sleep you need things to occupy your time. A mind needs to be exercised. It needs things to mull over. It's boring having nothing useful to do. It can drive you mad. At times like these there is the danger of the dead creating the most havoc. They have very little influence on the living but can force their hand when pushed to distraction.

Or, rather, they can force the hand of a witch, if they can find one.

A SHADE WITH A PURPOSE

He was certain it had been decades, maybe longer. Whenever it was he had handed in his mortal existence, he had no recollection. It was too long ago. One day he was in the form he now inhabited. There was no birth, no growing up. He just was.

Being alone all the time is not a lot of fun. It is, unfortunately, the price you pay for being dead. He was exceedingly bored. It is a common problem. Having nothing to do exacerbates the situation.

Only exercising the mind kills boredom. He had honed in on what he knew. There was one last piece of information stored deep in his psyche with which he could keep a tenuous hold on the physical world. He held onto that thought with all his might. He had set himself the goal to constantly focus on it and to never forget. Without it he was completely lost. It was like a single star flickering on a moonless night. It was the last remaining spark that could reignite his memory. Once it was gone, he feared the cogs of his mind would grind to a halt and everything would turn black.

What he knew hinged on one single detail: it was a she. She was of utmost importance. Who she was remained a mystery to him, yet the knowledge that she existed gave him the purpose he needed. Without her he was incomplete. He was truly in the dark. Something had happened somewhere, which had driven them apart. He wasn't sure who had been at fault for this. Perhaps an outside force had played a hand in it. He could only hypothesise. Only loose snippets of information floated around his mind. He tried to connect them all together, but couldn't. It was as if he was trying to solve a join-the-dots puzzle without having first learnt to count.

She was the love of his life. This was the one piece of the puzzle he knew for sure. Except, she was more than that. Love was a fleeting thing. The feeling he had went far beyond that. This love had staying power. Even in death it still called out to him. This was a love eternal. Something substantial had connected them. He didn't know what form it had taken, yet it was incredibly strong. It pulled from the other side. It was this love that drove him on. Because of it, he had no choice. It gave him purpose. He had to find her.

He had a picture of her in his head. It was just a sketch. She had dark hair. She was certainly older than him now, but had been younger than him when he had lived. The whole age thing was a bit clouded. She was still one of the living. He was certain of this. He sensed that the whole reason he was still around was because she lived. Otherwise, he surmised, his entire existence would be pointless. How could he solve this problem if the source of it no longer existed?

Physically he sensed they were about the same height now. If he were to stand in front of her, he could look her straight in the eye. He thought their features were somewhat similar. He looked once again at his reflection in the window, his real face. He ran his fingers around his chin. He had doubts. Maybe they weren't the same. He didn't know. He wasn't sure. The constant uncertainty was frustrating. He tried to create a mental image of her. He knotted his forehead and squeezed his eyes shut. It hurt his head, but couldn't conjure a clear image. It had been too long ago. He could only rely on instinct. He knew it wouldn't fail him. Instinct was all he had left. He was certain that when he found her, he would know she was the one.

He had tried to solve the mystery himself, but couldn't do it alone. He needed help. He had prowled the streets for what had seemed an eternity. As time whittled away, so did his memory. He felt the pressure growing. Time was of the essence and he was getting desperate. When he focussed on her it helped. Something told him there was perhaps more than one 'her'. Maybe this other her was the bridge, the doorway he was looking for, the solution that could help him out of his predicament.

He had looked for this other 'her', not realising she needed to be a witch. Right now, that witch was closer than he could possibly imagine.

THE PEOPLE PUZZLE

Events and people get shuffled around like one of those throwaway games you used to get at Christmas—a flat pad made up of tiles that have to be moved around and slotted into the right order to form a picture. They are called sliding puzzles. People and their actions follow similar principles.

As entities in a much bigger picture, we must keep shuffling our own stuff around until we find the right order. As in the sliding puzzle, the pieces we have are already in play and can't be lifted off the board. We have to shift them around until they make sense. They will have to find their natural place. It all boils down to patterns.

It's not simply one thing randomly following another. There are innumerable ways to order a sequence of events. It's complicated. Everything needs to be jostled around. At some stage all your pieces need to be used. Each piece borders another and thus all your individual components have to move and correspond to solve the puzzle. They also have to move in a certain way, one specific element after another. If you wish to see the end result, the picture, you need to find the correct sequence to put everything in its place. It is the law of the universe.

Nobody can disobey the laws of the universe. They are above everything. You might think you can go through life doing whatever you want. This is not so. Everything happens for a purpose. One thing leads to another. Action and reaction. You have to follow a series of patterns and you have to take all the steps. There are no shortcuts. In the beginning it doesn't matter which step you take. Later your alternatives become limited. If you want to find your end goal, your whole, if you want to see the big picture, you need to follow the law. You must find the right order. If not, then stuff just doesn't happen. The universe will not be happy. There will be no equilibrium, no balance.

And so it is that every occurrence in the universe has to happen. If that wasn't pressure enough, you must be aware that your time is limited. This is why we have the living and the dead. You get your chance to get it right while alive. Some of us have longer to do it than others, but if we stay the course there is time enough for all of us. Some of us will self-destruct before we get there. This manifests itself in various fashions. It doesn't have to be as cut and dried as suicide. We all have choices. We all have a hand in our own mortality. Nobody gets off lightly. We all have to put in some semblance of effort. The universe doesn't accept notes from your mum or other lame excuses. We all have to do the work.

For some, this is a serious problem. They get stuck.

The universe doesn't care. It will wait. It won't let you go until you have solved the puzzle. Eventually, every single one of your pieces will need to be slotted in its place. If not, you will be required to hang around for longer than planned until that happens.

Shades haven't finished putting everything in place. They still have loose components that need to slide into position. Don't think for a minute that being dead excuses you from your duties. No way. You have no one to blame but yourself. You've still got to do whatever it is you were meant to do. Unfortunately, you've just made the job that much harder by going and getting yourself killed.

There is no hell. There is only unfinished business.

PURPLE RAIN

There was something about him that caught her attention. For some reason he was always hanging out in front of Kentucky Fried Chicken. Anaïs had seen him there on numerous occasions. It was as though he had lost his way. Well, they all had. She knew that shades were trying to find an open door to the next world. Some of them found it by themselves and some of them needed help.

One of the most important directives of The Organisation was that, wherever possible, all members were required to help shades find their way. Not being able to communicate directly with them made it something of a chore. It was a directive that was not intentionally neglected, but did slip down the list of priorities. Some witches set it high on their agendas. There were the odd Mother Teresas of witchdom who made it their life's work to care exclusively for shades. They were in the minority, and most did not feel compelled to fulfil this obligation on a full-time basis.

P J WHITTLESEA

Anaïs fell into this group. She was still working her way through puberty, and the needs of others were far from her mind. And boy, puberty was taking a long time.

It really screwed with her head. She dreaded to think what it would be like when her body caught up and she was lumped with physical transformations as well. The brain drain was enough. It was driving her to distraction. All she seemed to do was think about boys. She was obsessed with them. Every teenager on the verge of growing facial hair grabbed her attention. She couldn't keep her eyes off them.

That had been the primary drawing power of Kentucky Fried Chicken. It was full of boys. Most of the other hang-out options involved hamburgers. Anaïs didn't like hamburgers.

Why this particular shade was hanging around outside Kentucky Fried Chicken was a mystery to Anaïs. He was as dead as they come. Perhaps it was the smell of fried chicken; a lingering memory from his time among the living. It certainly wasn't hunger. Shades didn't eat. She was concerned that his continued appearance in front of the display window would draw unnecessary attention. It could produce a sticky situation if the store manager or, even worse, the police or a security guard, were to try to communicate with him.

Regrettably, she knew it was her duty to protect him. She would try to establish a line of communication.

She frowned. He was singing.

'Doo, do, do, do, dooo. Doo, do, do, do, dooo. Doo, do di do dooo.'

He didn't seem to notice her standing there. She was

used to that. She was sure she could stand there for hours and wouldn't be noticed. He made her smile. He was funny. He was so preoccupied.

He stared at his reflection in the plate glass window.

'Doo, do, do, do, dooo. Doo, do, do, do, dooo. Doo, do di do dooo.'

The dead can't talk. It's not that they can't converse in any way at all, but you need to find other ways, apart from the spoken word, to establish a rapport. It can be a laborious task, trying to get anything sensible out of them. Some of the dead are better at conversing than others. Finding a good communicator is a godsend. If there is a hint that discourse is possible, there is already something of a foundation to build the witch-shade relationship on. All relationships work the same way. In most you will encounter difficulties at some stage. Relationships between the living and the dead are no exception. Although they do come with their own special set of complications.

This shade could sing, or at least hum a tune. This is a rare talent among the dead. There are a few in every city. They hum the whole day through and the living hear it. It is infectious. Everybody has experienced the moment when some irritatingly simple hit song enters their brain. As long as you are fixated on the tune it won't leave you. It can be quite irritating. Under most circumstances, these pearls of songwriting are introduced by one of those rogue shades with singing abilities—although some may prefer to see it as a disability. It is one of the few ways shades can influence the living. Thankfully the dead don't know the power they hold in their hands and have not taken advantage of it. If they were to do so, the earth's entire population would be walking around with stupid songs stuck in their heads. It would be a disaster, pandemonium; chaos would reign supreme. In the extreme, wars would break out. People would resort to anything to get the damn things out of their heads.

'Doo, do, do, do, dooo. Doo, do, do, do, dooo. Doo, do di do dooo.'

Anaïs knew the tune. It was one of Nan's favourite songs, by her favourite artist. Nan would sit for hours swooning at the album cover like a school girl. She put the song on all the time. The melody was etched into Anaïs's brain. She didn't mind the song but, more importantly, there was also a very crucial colour connection.

Nan really loved Prince's 'Purple Rain'.

Anaïs checked the street around her. Thankfully no one had noticed them, but it wouldn't take long. She had to warn him that he was running the risk of attracting attention. His camouflage was solid. Yet she caught glimpses of other things. She could see his facial expressions and other movements. He was on the verge of breaking out into an air-guitar solo. Maybe others could see it too. That just wouldn't do. She had to stop him.

'Hello,' she said.

He didn't notice her. He was still staring blankly at his reflection in the window, swaying from side to side and singing to himself.

Anaïs raised her voice. 'Hello!'

This time he heard her and it made him jump. He stopped singing and looked furtively around him. Then he looked down. There was panic in his eyes and he was clearly startled to see her looking directly up at him. He turned his head away and back again, checking if he really was the centre of attention. He was.

Anaïs eyeballed him. 'Hello,' she said again.

Nobody had ever communicated directly with him. He looked around again. The street was busy but no one seemed to notice them. That was normal, though: no one ever paid attention to him. He ignored the street and concentrated solely on her. She held her ground and looked up at him with sparkling eyes. Just looking at her made him feel better. She was a tiny beauty.

He had tried to talk to people over the years. No one ever heard him. At times and out of pure frustration, he had screamed at the top of his lungs. The living never responded. The division between his world and theirs was rock-solid. They saw one thing and it wasn't the real him. He could pull faces or even stand on his head. It didn't make any difference. The living only ever saw the shell. The disguise blocked everything. It was exasperating.

So how was it that she had spotted him? Could she

see the real him? Was she not a mortal? Was she dead like him? He thought he had seen other shades before, but he wasn't certain. He had sensed them. He also thought he had caught sight of their reflections, but there was no way to communicate. What he had seen were merely fragments, usually out of the corner of his eye. He had seen the same familiar behaviour he himself portrayed, being ignored by the rest of the world. Just like him, they had also been jumping around in their skins. He had reached out to some of them but they never responded. He doubted that anything he did would ever work. Long ago he had given up trying and resigned himself to his solitary existence. Trying was a waste of energy and had frustrated him no end. Even thinking about it depressed him.

There was something special about her, though. She could see him. She had tried to talk to him. He had to make an effort in return. He decided not to yell and scream. Being over-enthusiastic might frighten her. He would just talk normally.

He spoke quietly and heard his voice squeak. He hadn't used it in such a long time. He cleared his throat but what came out was still a croak, *'Hello yourself.'*

Now it was her turn to be surprised. She stepped away from him. 'Say that again?'

His eyes darted from side to side in uncertainty. He wet his lips and heard his chest creak as he tried to fill his dormant lungs. *'Hello yourself.'*

She beamed and shook her fists in jubilation. 'I can hear you!'

He was pleased and shocked all at once. This was

truly exciting. He tried to maintain his composure. He didn't want to scare her away. Not that she could read his face anyway. Or could she do that too?

'Wow! Really?'

'Yes, in here.' She tapped the side of her skull with the tips of her fingers.

'Who are you?'

'Anaïs, Anaïs Thistle. And you?'

'I honestly don't know.'

'Oh, that's a shame. Do you know what I am?'

'No.'

'I'm a witch.' She proudly puffed up her chest. 'I've been told I can do this, you know, communicate with you guys and all, but I've never been successful at it. Nan tells me it's what I'm meant to do.' She took a step back and looked him up and down. A smile split her face and she shook her head. 'Wow! Nobody ever responded to me before. It's as if they couldn't see me.'

'I know the feeling. I've had a similar experience,' he said flatly.

Suddenly he was overcome with emotion. He leant forward, supporting his weight with his hands on his knees. Tears welled up in his eyes and a single teardrop escaped and ran along the bridge of his nose to the tip. She saw it and reached up to brush it away. A spark jumped off her hand when she touched him and a tremor ran through his body. He felt weak at the knees and crouched down beside her. Now that he was on her level he looked her square in the eye.

'I've never been able to do this before either, actually talk to someone. Nobody ever hears me. You're the first.' He sniffed and

dried his face with his sleeve. *'You don't know how much I appreciate this. Thank you for listening. It's been hell not being able to communicate with anyone.'*

'It's ok. There's no need to thank me. Like I said, it's a first for me as well.' She was so excited she couldn't stand still. She shuffled on the spot. 'Oooh, it's so cool.' She glowed at him. 'I need to call you something. You must have a name. What is it?'

He shook his head. *'A name? I don't know. I never had any use for one before.'*

'Oh, that's a shame. We'll have to do something about that.' Anaïs thought for a moment. She scratched her head and then stopped. 'I know, let's give you one. Do you have any ideas?'

He shook his head.

She looked down at her feet and then her face lit up. 'You were humming something before.'

'Really, you could hear that?'

'Yes, it's strange. I can't hear you speaking out loud, but I did hear that. You were humming "Purple Rain". It's one of my favourites. You see, I really, really, like purple.' She screwed up her face. 'Do you know Prince?'

'Yes, I know him. Not personally, you know. He's an ok musician. I like music. If I didn't have music to listen to, I don't know what I would do.'

She put her hands on her hips. 'Well, then it's settled. We'll just call you that.'

'What? Purple Rain?'

'No, don't be silly.' Anaïs laughed at him. 'We'll call you Prince.'

His eyes flashed with delight. She grinned back at him.

It was strange to think that he finally had an identity. Years of wandering aimlessly had brought nothing. He had lost all sense of time. He had resigned himself to his pointless existence. But that was now over. He had an identity. Sure, it was borrowed, but it was better than nothing. It was a gift, the best gift he could ever recall being given. In fact, it was the only gift he could remember receiving. Not only that, he now had someone to talk to. He struggled to form the words.

'Thank you,' he said.

She smiled broadly at him and, as she did, he felt a new energy course through his body. It was a wondrous day.

TAKING THE DEAD HOME

'What have I told you about hanging around with strangers?'

Anaïs sighed. 'Not to do it?'

'Exactly,' said Nan. 'So why are you doing it?'

Nan had been relieved to find her, especially because she wasn't where she should have been. She had looked for Anaïs inside Kentucky Fried Chicken but couldn't find her. For a moment she had feared the worst; that someone had taken her. Her heart had pounded and she had become flushed with worry. It had taken everything in her power to halt the urge to panic. She had managed to calm herself. Nan had wandered between the tables hoping to find Anaïs hiding in a corner somewhere, but she was nowhere to be found. Nan had widened her search. She'd scanned the restaurant one last time and then spotted them. Through the big show window she saw them standing outside, next to the entrance. She swore under her breath.

'I felt sorry for him.' Anaïs and Prince stood next to each other like two children who had just been punished. They looked at Nan with puppy eyes, their arms hanging in submission at their sides. Nan cursed at the way she was so defenceless against the little witch's begging. It was her responsibility to manage Anaïs, but those eyes got her every time. Something about them always floored her. Sometimes she forgot she was really dealing with a teenager. Anaïs often flaunted her physical talents to get her way and Nan reminded herself of this. A pouting five-year-old was capable of demanding attention, but Anaïs wasn't a preschooler anymore.

The old man was another thing altogether. Nan couldn't see his real eyes. To her, his visage was deadpan. He was staring straight through her and blankly into space. The old man was completely catatonic and appeared to be suffering from senility. He swayed slightly and looked unsteady on his feet. He didn't even seem to notice her standing there. She wondered if he was sober.

'And he's special,' said Anaïs.

'Is he now?' Nan growled at her. 'I'm not sure I can see that.'

Anaïs thought for a moment and realised her caretaker was right. Nan couldn't see what she saw. She straightened and gave her a serious look. 'He's dead, Nan. He's a shade.'

Nan caught her breath. 'Oh.'

She was not prepared for this. It took her by

surprise. The Organisation had trained her extensively, but this was the first time she had met a shade. Her training deserted her. She was at a loss about how to handle the situation, and Nan was rarely at a loss about anything.

She tried to compose herself and give the impression everything was normal. Except it wasn't. Hanging out with a dead person in the middle of a crowded street was far from normal. She looked around self-consciously. No one seemed to pay them any attention. To a passerby, there was nothing special about them. They looked like any small family unit standing in front of a restaurant and possibly trying to decide what they wanted for lunch.

Nan looked him up and down. He was unresponsive but didn't look dead. Then something caught her eye. She looked at his feet. He appeared to be floating and didn't seem to be connected to the ground. Then she realised what it was: he had no shadow. She took a deep breath and slowly exhaled. Keeping one eye on the shade she turned to Anaïs.

'What do you want to do with him?' she asked.

Anaïs pondered the question. 'I think he needs my help. Actually, I'm certain he needs my help. I can feel it. It's my responsibility, remember?'

Nan nodded. She was fully aware of The Organisation's directives. She knew exactly what it meant, only it was new to her and she hadn't been prepared for such a sudden shift in direction. She needed to make a mental adjustment. The time had come. Anaïs had a task to fulfil and Nan's job was to assist.

School was out, the training was over, and now it was happening for real.

A HOUSE GUEST

'Wait a minute,' Nan snapped at her. 'You can't bring him inside.'

Anaïs sneered at her. 'He's not a dog.'

Nan was emphatic. 'As far as I'm concerned, he might as well be. He creeps me out. He just stares into space and I have no idea what he's thinking. He bugs me. Get him out of here. I need time to think.'

Nan stood on the landing in front of the door to their apartment with the keys hanging in her hands. She waited.

Anaïs wasn't going to give up without a fight. 'But where should I put him?'

'I don't care, as long as it's not in here.' She jangled the keys in the direction of the apartment door.

Anaïs looked forlornly at Prince. He shrugged his shoulders.

'It's ok. I'll hang outside.'

'But it's freezing,' she protested.

'Anaïs, it's ok. I don't feel anything. Well, I don't feel the cold. I do feel other things, though.' He shot a wicked look at Nan who failed to see anything because of his camouflage.

Nan looked at Anaïs and then at Prince. 'You mean you can talk to him?'

Anaïs nodded.

'And he talks to you? You hear him?'

She pointed at her temple. 'Only in my head.' Her eyes lit up. 'Oh, and I can hear him humming.'

'Humming?' Nan was exasperated. She blew out an invisible candle. 'Look, he can stay outside, but he has to hide. I won't have him hanging around outside the house. He'll attract too much attention.'

'How am I supposed to hide him?'

'Give him a blanket, then he'll look like all the other homeless bums.'

'You have no compassion.'

'No, you're right,' said Nan with a hint of sarcasm. 'I used it all up on you.'

'Sheesh!'

Anaïs grabbed him by the hand. 'Come on, let's find you somewhere to hide.'

Nan was horrified. 'What are you doing? Don't touch him! He's dead for God's sake!'

Anaïs pulled a face. 'He's a shade, not a rotting corpse.'

Nan twisted her lip. 'Whatever! It's just the thought of it.'

'Since when did you get all queasy about such things.'

'It's not a new development,' said Nan. 'We don't usually have them in such close quarters. Most of the dead people I know are under the ground.'

Anaïs chose to ignore her comment and went to lead Prince back down the stairs. He stopped her.

'It's not necessary to go with me. I'll find somewhere.' He noted the concerned look on her face. *'I'm used to having to fend for myself. Don't worry about me, Anaïs. I won't go far.'*

She looked up at him. 'Are you sure?'

He smiled at her with his eyes. *'Of course. I'm glad I finally found someone to talk to. I'm not going anywhere fast. I'll be outside if you need me.'*

Anaïs smiled at him. 'I don't think I'll be needing you but it's good to know. It makes a nice change to have someone new to talk to.' She flipped a finger over her shoulder. 'I'm getting kind of sick of her.'

Nan raised an eyebrow as she fumbled with the keys in the lock. 'Oh, nice, thank you very much.' There was no disguising her sarcastic tone. She opened the door and stood in the doorway waiting for Anaïs.

Anaïs ignored her. Prince reluctantly let go of her hand. He walked across the small landing and descended the narrow staircase. For the first time Anaïs realised that he made no sound. The noisy stairs, which usually creaked and groaned with every step, were silent. She leant over the bannister. As he turned to step down the next flight of stairs he looked up. He winked at her and she smiled back. She was reassured he wouldn't go far. She followed Nan into their apartment and closed the door behind her.

'Thank you,' said Nan. 'I don't know what it is but he unnerves me.'

Anaïs grudgingly accepted the apology. 'Fine.'

'Are you hungry?' Nan tried to change the subject. 'I'll make us something to eat.'

Anaïs sulked. 'Maybe.'

PREVENTING THE TEMPEST

itches try to avoid congregating together. If there are too many of them in one location, the concentration of their powers becomes excessive. It affects nature. The witch population is better off thinly spread.

Thunderstorms are generally the best indication that too many witches are in the same area. If they are too slow in becoming aware of the presence of other witches nearby, the storm will worsen. In the extreme, this can lead to cyclones and tornados. Witches are creatures of comfort and prefer a warm climate, so even though steps are taken to ensure safe distances, there is a disproportionate amount of electrical activity around the equator.

One of the most important directives of The Organisation is that witches are sworn to protect the human population from undue harm. Damage limitation is the fundamental aim and occupation of the witch community. If harm has already come to something, then it's a lot more difficult to repair. If extreme destruction has occurred it can be impossible to return things to normal.

The easiest way to stop this sort of thing happening is through prevention. If a dangerous situation can be avoided, that is preferred above anything else.

If the witch community had its way, they would enclose the entire population of the world in impregnable cocoons. That way they wouldn't be obliged to keep a watchful eye on everyone all the time.

It's important to note that witches are not responsible for human acts of stupidity. Anything self-inflicted is not their problem, it's yours. So if you feel the urge to jump off the side of a mountain with a handkerchief to slow your fall, or if you decide to rely on a tank of air to sustain you hundreds of metres under water, then you do it at your own risk. Don't expect a witch to jump in and save you if something goes horribly wrong. They have better things to do. They have their own priorities.

Witches are like most *Homo sapiens*: they are prone to laziness. If a job can be avoided, it will be at all costs. Nobody wants to spend every waking hour working. We all cherish our free time and prefer to just have fun. There is also a limited numbers of witches. They can't be everywhere at all times.

If a witch were to create an unwanted situation, then she would also be responsible for setting things back on track. Performing damage restoration costs an inordinate amount of time, and most of them have better things to do.

In short, prevention is a much more efficient course of action. Not only that, it requires and consumes a lot less energy.

A VISITOR

The first change Anaïs noticed was the wind.

It's quite common to get gale-force winds in Amsterdam, especially in certain seasons. The Netherlands is a flat land and there are few obstacles to block the ferocious, northerly, Arctic blast. Only, it was midwinter and this kind of wind was odd. It generally reserved itself for the onset of spring.

Anaïs's attention was drawn to it by the scraping of branches on the window. She rested her forehead against the glass and looked out from their second-floor apartment. The leafless tree outside the window struggled to maintain its form. Its thin branches grasped at the air. She watched as a particularly strong gust swept down the street. The force toppled a scooter on the other side of the street. Its windshield shattered as it crashed to the ground and made a terrible sound.

The street was deserted except for one person. On the opposite footpath stood a woman in a long, heavy, fur-lined pelisse. She stood not far from the fallen scooter and had been unmoved by its collapse. Her coat whipped around her legs, slapping her knee-high boots. She held a wide-brimmed hat down over her ears with both hands. Her face was obscured and she appeared to be studying the ground between her feet. Leaves and other bits of rubbish swirled around her ankles and spiralled into the air above her. Everything was in motion except for her. It was as if the wind was drawing itself into her. She stood her ground firmly, swaying slightly every now and then as each fresh blast buffeted her.

Anaïs looked up and down the street in search of Prince but he was nowhere to be seen. She wondered where he had hidden himself. She looked up at the sky. Dark clouds were forming. She shivered and pulled her vest tightly around her torso. Its thin layer wasn't warm enough. She walked back to her chair and retrieved her overcoat. She pulled it on and drew the collar in snugly around her neck.

'That's better,' she said and startled herself with her own voice.

She went back to the window. The woman had gone. Anaïs shrugged. She sat down, leant on the table in front of her and tapped its surface impatiently with her fingernails. A vase with a large bunch of flowers stood in the middle of the table. The smell was overpowering. Nan was always buying flowers and the house was filled with them. It was yet another idiosyncrasy which irritated Anaïs about her caretaker. Sometimes it felt as though she was living in a funeral parlour. To spite Nan, Anaïs reached out and pulled the petals off one of the flowers.

A fresh gust of wind caused the branches of the tree outside to slam hard against the window. It gave her a start and she almost toppled the vase by jerking too hard on a petal, which remained securely attached to its host. She released her grip on the flowers, straightened the vase and resumed her tapping on the table.

She hoped the wind would die down. She wanted to go out and spend more time with Prince. It was supposed to be a fine, sunny day. The view outside contradicted this. Nan was in the kitchen preparing lunch. She would ask her about the weather forecast when she came in. Her tapping was interrupted by the rumble of distant thunder.

So much for the sunshine, she thought.

The doorbell buzzed loudly. Once again, she jumped in her seat. The caller held the button in impatiently and much longer than necessary. Its coarse, electric vibration grated on her ears. A piece of cutlery clattered to the kitchen floor. Nan cursed. Anaïs heard her leave the kitchen and slide down the corridor on her slippers with a swishing sound.

'Ok! I'm coming!'

Anaïs heard Nan fumble with the lock and open the door. There was a moment of silence, and then some murmuring followed by the sound of a scuffle. Nan's shrill voice rang out. 'No! Stop!'

The living room door swung wide open and hit the wall with a loud thud. The woman she had seen out in the street filled the doorway. Her wide hat, a fedora, still sat low on her head but her pale face was now clearly visible. It shone out from beneath the brim, as did her eyes. There was a look of desperation in them. They seemed to glow brightly in the shadows under the hat, with almost entirely white orbs except for the tiny, black pinpoints of her pupils.

The woman bellowed, 'You have to stop what you're doing.'

Anaïs made herself small, shrank back into her chair and squeaked, 'What?'

'You're endangering all of us.' The woman's chest heaved. 'Stop using my name.'

She stepped forward into the room and suddenly seemed to forget what she was doing. Her anger dissipated and the look on her face softened. Her intense eyes dimmed and a sadness came over her. 'Oh, I've missed you so much.'

Anaïs was confused. *Who was this person?*

The woman moved towards her. Over her shoulder Anaïs caught a glimpse of Nan bursting into the room behind her. She lunged at the woman. 'No! Don't!'

The woman dodged Nan, pushed the table aside, sending the vase crashing to the floor, and drew Anaïs into her arms. Her heavy coat completely engulfed the little witch and shrouded everything in darkness. An incredible warmth exuded from the woman. It flushed her own body like a fever. The woman clasped the child's head firmly to her chest and Anaïs heard the rapid thump of her heart. And then there was nothing; only silence.

Anaïs felt the air around her suck in like a vacuum

and squeeze her entire body. The woman's coat enveloped her like a leotard. It held her momentarily in a tight hug before releasing its grip. A minuscule pinprick of intense bright light appeared in the darkness, floating in front of her eyes. It swelled and expanded instantaneously into a blinding flash. All she saw was white. There was an enormous explosion. The noise popped her eardrums and left her deafened. The floor gave way. For the longest moment she floated, hanging in nothingness, and then she followed the floor's descent. She felt herself plummet.

There was a second explosion, and a rush of air from one side. She changed direction. She was no longer moving vertically but horizontally. Her falling became flying. She was completely disorientated. She swung her arms blindly in empty space. She was now alone, the woman gone.

She stopped grasping at the air and let the momentum of her flight propel her. Then she hit something solid—the ground—and instinctively rolled into a ball. She spun around and around, bouncing like a beach ball. Then she felt a blow to her spine. The fallen scooter across the street had brought her to a halt.

With the bright flash, she had involuntarily closed her eyes. Tentatively, she now opened them. Lying on her side and seeking shelter, she pressed herself up close and under the scooter. She watched as the building across the street crumpled in on itself. The noise was tremendous, like the roar of cannon-fire. A cloud of dust billowed outwards and upwards and swept across the street towards her. She covered her mouth and pinched her nostrils with one hand.

From the corner of her eye she saw part of the neighbouring building break off. It fell in on what remained of her house and added to the expanding pall. She held her breath and slung her free arm over her head to protect herself from any stray debris. Pulling her knees up under her chin, she cowered up against the scooter and waited for it all to subside.

CHANGING A NAME

N ames are special things. They attach themselves to people. Nowadays, most people are given names before they are even born. In some cultures, the sighting of an animal or some other occurrence in the vicinity of the unborn child, results in them being named after it. The Fins are one of the few peoples on the planet who actually wait for a time after the child is born before settling on a name. This is an admirable quality but doesn't quite explain why many Finnish names end in an 'i'. You would think that the extra time would give them the opportunity to come up with something more experimental. But then, spending half the year in complete darkness and freezing temperatures probably plays havoc with the imagination.

There are other countries, such as Germany, where you are only allowed to choose from a set list of names. You are not permitted to make them up. This is an unfortunate thing in a country with so many people. It explains why so many of them carry the same name. Quite often, Germans end up using a last name or a nickname to associate with individuals. There's no other way around it. It's not unusual to find yourself in a room full of Peters. When in Germany, you must resort to alternative names if you want to call someone out of a crowd. Otherwise, you will have the uncomfortable situation where, when you yell out a name, the entire room turns to face you.

Witches are not strictly human and do not adhere to the laws of earthly beings. No two witches have the same name. Admittedly, there aren't nearly as many witches as Germans. Therefore, witches do have a numbers advantage. This makes it possible to have a truly unique name for every witch on the planet. Their names are more than merely a collection of letters. They carry a certain weight. They are powerful.

Witches and other beings of a mystical persuasion are named before they are even conceived. A name exists and then the seed of a child is attached to it. In some ways the name is more important than the one who will bear it. Long before the person who will be its bearer is even thought of, the name is there. In some way, this is actually similar in the sublunary world. Only, as with many things when comparing the two worlds, it is in reverse. For naturals in modern times, once someone has left this world their name lives on forever. Witches' names have preceded them since the dawn of time.

Ancient indigenous cultures were more knowledgeable about this and followed principles similar to witches. They knew the importance of names. They practised that a name was buried with a person. Once someone perished, or vacated the earthly realm, the name must never again be spoken aloud. Because of the extreme explosion of life on the planet, this has become impractical. There are only so many names in existence. Or perhaps there are not. Perhaps, just like the Germans, we are being too cautious and need to think outside the box.

Witches are products of an ancient culture and therefore adhere to the practice of letting a name die with its physical attachment. A name and a person are isolated yet connected entities. For witches there is great esteem attached to being bestowed with a name. As its bearer you have a responsibility to it. It is yours and yours alone. No one else can have the honour of owning it. Naturally there are individual names that are shared. It is the combination of names that make them particular to one person.

There are no nameless witches. There are those who should never be mentioned, but that is different. You find them everywhere. There are always bad eggs. But a witch without a name is no longer an entity. Once attached to a witch, where the name goes, so does the body. In the same way, if there is no name, then there will no longer be a body.

Nobody knows the full ramifications of tampering with names, but the consequences are potentially dire.

CONSEQUENCES

naïs was distraught. She couldn't find Nan.

The building had collapsed with such completeness that nothing but a massive pile of rubble remained. Anaïs was certain that Nan was under it somewhere. She had to find her. She began to scale the ruins. The dust had not yet fully settled and she coughed on a mouthful of it. Underfoot, the mass of bricks and concrete was loose and unstable. She had trouble securing her footing. She took off her beret and searched around in it. She quickly found what she was looking for and pulled it out. A drinking straw. It was no ordinary drinking straw. She stuck it in her mouth and breathed slowly in and out through it. It filtered the air.

She calmed herself and, after a few deep gulps of fresh air, regulated her breathing. She reached into her jacket pocket and pulled out her promptuary. Opening it, she pulled the straw out of her mouth for a moment.

'Heat seeker,' she said.

She put the straw back into her mouth and stared into the book. The white page flickered and morphed into a black screen. A soft humming came from the promptuary. She held it out in front of her with both hands and used it to scan her surroundings. She spun in a circle, slowly raising and lowering the book as she went in order to cover everything around her. She stopped when the humming rose in pitch. A faint white dot appeared on the screen.

With straw in mouth, and holding the promptuary in front of her in one hand, she clambered over the debris. To an observer it looked as if it was leading her by the hand. The humming continued to rise in pitch and the small white dot grew in size until it practically filled the black screen. She stopped and looked down at her feet. There was something warm under her. She hoped it was Nan. She couldn't be sure, but was fairly certain no one else had been in the building. She dropped the promptuary into her coat pocket and bent down to examine the spot. A noise caught her ear and she looked up.

A crowd had begun to gather on the edge of the demolished building. She tapped into her own genuine fear and trepidation and burst into tears. For once it wasn't difficult to play the role of a distraught child.

'Help!' she cried, 'there's someone under here.'

Two men immediately broke from the crowd and scrabbled up onto the brickwork. When they reached her, she stood back and pointed forlornly at the rubble beneath her feet. The men sank to their knees and groped at the broken fragments of concrete and brick where she had indicated. They tossed the debris aside and worked their way deeper. One of them stopped, wiped his mouth with his sleeve and spat out a gob of wet dust. It slapped a slab of concrete lying about a metre away. It stuck out of the rubble at a rank angle like a tombstone.

'There's a leg,' he said to his accomplice.

'Quick!' said the other man.

Together they dived back into the rubble and enlarged the hole. Then they both stopped and leant back. One of them held up his hand, signalling Anaïs not to approach.

'Don't look,' he said.

She ignored his advice and stepped forward. Leaning with her chest on his open palm, she looked over his shoulder. Nan's crumpled body lay broken across a bed of bricks. Her limbs were twisted but her beautiful face was untouched. Only her body was an empty shell, and lifeless.

Both men turned to face Anaïs. 'We're too late,' one of them said apologetically.

She struggled to process his words. In desperation she looked around and then down at what was left of Nan. She blubbered and a faint whine grew at the back of her throat.

'No!'

Anaïs's high-pitched scream punched the air and reverberated off the surrounding buildings. She let herself fall backwards and sat down heavily, jarring the base of her spine on the sharp edge of a brick. She didn't feel it. She felt nothing except an excruciating pain in her chest. The scream had drained her lungs. She couldn't breathe. Everything was tied up. She tried to inhale and choked. Then she remembered the straw. She jammed it in her mouth, gasped, and coaxed her lungs into action. Air flowed and she let out a loud sob.

One of the men clambered up out of the hole. He swept her up in his arms and held her tightly. Her body shook in his grip as he stumbled across the ruins with her. She buried her face deep in the crook of his arm and wept.

For once she was grateful she was trapped in the body of a little girl. Now, she was free to act like one.

Prince watched from a distant edge of the ruins as the crowd converged around Anaïs. He felt useless. It had all transpired before him but he had been rooted to the spot by shock. It had happened so fast. One minute he had been sheltering in the recessed entrance of a nearby building. The next, he had watched as her building collapsed.

Before it had disintegrated and folded in on itself, he had seen Anaïs fly out of the carnage. He had watched her stand up after the razing had subsided and it surprised him that she was completely unharmed.

There was nothing he could do. He wanted to comfort her but couldn't. He couldn't force his way into the crowd. They would think it strange if she communicated with a mute old man. He doubted that she would be ready to receive any words of reassurance from him anyway. The shock would have to dissipate.

He would wait. That was something he was very good at.

A DEATH IN THE FAMILY

'*What have you done?*' Prince knew he should console her but his mind was clouded with anger.

As he waited he had mulled over what had happened and came to the conclusion that his goal might be put in jeopardy. How could Anaïs help him without the assistance of a fully-fledged mortal? He became exasperated by the whole situation. He felt the chance he had been offered slipping through his hands.

Ambulance personnel had checked Anaïs and decided that, except for the shock of the event, she was fine. They left her sitting on the rear step of the ambulance and went to see if anyone else needed assistance. Prince took the opportunity to draw her away from the scene. Together they had slipped around the corner and into the next street. She had gone willingly as his was the only familiar face she knew. She had nowhere else to go.

'I didn't do anything,' she retorted.

Prince was ropeable. *'Yes, you did. What just happened was all your fault.'*

'No it wasn't. How is that possible?'

'She wouldn't have turned up if you hadn't summoned her.'

'I didn't summon her, I swear.'

'No, not on purpose, I suppose, but that is irrelevant.'

'Since when did you become an expert on all things witchlike?'

'I don't need to be. I have ears. She said you stole her name.'

Anaïs had to think but it was difficult. Her head was still in turmoil from everything that had happened. *Was he right? Did she say that?* She tried to focus and replayed the few moments in the living room through her mind. *He was right. The woman did say it. She said, 'Stop using my name.'*

'Oh.' Anaïs sucked on her lower lip. She began to cry. Through her tears she looked up at Prince. He carried his usual stone-face and his eyes offered no sympathy. She dropped her own eyes to the ground and sulked.

The fluttering of wings made her look up again. A pigeon flew down and alighted on his shoulder. It lifted its tail feathers and proceeded to defecate down his arm. Anaïs screwed up her face. 'Eeeuw!'

Prince vigorously shook his arm. The bird held on with its talons, flapped its wings and then hopped down onto his forearm. It looked straight at Anaïs and inquired with a deep, calm voice, 'Miss Blue?'

Anaïs sniffed, rubbed her eyes with the palms of her hands and smeared her tears across her face. She snorted and wiped her running nose on the back of her sleeve. She looked first at the bird and then up at Prince. 'Did you say something?'

Prince shook his head. His eyes darted down to the bird on his arm, indicating where the sound had come from.

'Miss Anaïs Blue?'

Anaïs was perplexed. She stared at the bird. 'Yes?'

The pigeon lifted one leg and pulled at a metal tube attached to it with its beak. 'Could you help me, please?' it said.

Anaïs looked at Prince and he shrugged.

'Sure,' she said.

Prince leant forward and she reached out and gently pried at the tube. She removed a piece of rolled up paper from behind it and unfolded it.

Block letters were printed on it: PLEASE INSERT IN PROMPTUARY.

She pulled out her handbook, opened it and laid the thin paper along the spine. The paper rolled itself into a ball, grew in size and floated above the page. It began to glow and transformed into a bright sphere in the form of a small sun.

'Thank you, pigeon,' the sun boomed in a voice identical to the bird's.

Prince and Anaïs watched the bird adjust the tube around its leg with its beak, and then it took off. They both took a step back to avoid being hit and watched it fly off between the buildings. They then turned their attention back to the ball of light hovering above the handbook.

It thundered, 'Your presence is requested

immediately. Please follow the light. You may close your handbook.'

Anaïs did as requested and shut the book. The ball of light detached itself from the promptuary and hovered between the two of them. Anaïs pocketed her handbook. Slowly the mini sun began moving and they followed it.

As they walked back down the street Anaïs caught a final glimpse of the carnage around the corner. She hesitated, closing her eyes, before moving on. The image of Nan's inert body lying in the rubble returned to her. She shuddered and an immense sadness came over her. Her greatest regret was not having the chance to properly say her farewells.

A NEW KIND OF DARKNESS

There are many kinds of darkness.

Some kinds of darkness cannot be seen but still have a tactile form. They can certainly be felt. There is one particular darkness that goes deeper than any other and is more akin to blackness than any perception of day or night. The realm of supreme blackness, of tenebrosity. Known as The Brotherhood, it had one particularly loyal servant. He was known simply as the Inquisitor.

The universe has to have balance. There is no up without down, no night without day, and no good without evil. For all the positive aspects of witches there also has to be a negative force that holds it all in check. Pure goodness cannot exist without an opposite pole to reveal what is truly good.

Every man's good is subjective. The Inquisitor believed what he was doing was virtuous. It was his ordained task. It was honourable. He was charged with protecting the living from the unknown. Unfortunately, for those really in the know, all he basically did was make an already difficult job more complicated. Any action he undertook would be pernicious.

Anaïs had heard of The Brotherhood but had never paid much attention to them. They had never threatened her. She was a secret and existed in a realm concealed deep beneath their radar. Nan and The World Witch Organisation had kept her sheltered. Her disguise had been immaculate. Now that their house had collapsed, so had the shroud which had made her invisible. Unbeknownst to Anaïs, she had drawn attention to herself. She was now at risk.

The populous in the city of Amsterdam were also oblivious to the reality of what had just happened, all except for one man. Right now he surveyed the ruined buildings from the opposite side of the street. He stood in the exact position in which the mysterious woman had stood. He wasn't looking at the rescue workers picking through the rubble. He was focussed on something lying on the ground between his feet.

The Inquisitor bent down and picked it up. It was a piece of black cloth, the torn corner of a coat.

He took out a cigarette lighter and tried to set fire to it. It wouldn't burn. He inspected it closely and saw a curious gold thread running along the seam. He flexed and folded the cloth and placed it in the palm of his hand. He watched as it uncreased itself and returned to its original flattened form.

He turned the piece of cloth thoughtfully over in his fingers. It was a clue.

A SHADE WITH ATTITUDE

There was something about him that she couldn't quite place. He carried himself differently. Most shades wandered around in a dreamlike-state. He didn't do that. He had purpose.

He stood stock-still, in the middle of the crowded street, on the other side of the road. The late-afternoon shoppers were out and the city was busy. People were running around, trying to cram in everything they had to do before the stores closed. The shade ignored them. Like a tree in a storm, he was immovable and rooted to the ground. The wind of the crowd swirled wildly around him. He was completely unruffled. He was focused. He was staring blankly straight ahead. Or was he?

He was not gazing into nothingness. He was looking at something in particular. He was staring directly at her. Anaïs felt exposed and looked around to see if anyone else had noticed her and Prince. No one had. He was the only one. He had singled them out. There was something in his eyes, in the intensity of his look, that unsettled her. He wore thick-lensed glasses that magnified his eyes, heightening the effect of his stare.

There was an overtly pushy air about him. She felt it from where she stood. He wanted her, and only her. And he wasn't willing to wait. But why was she so special? And what was his urgency? It was irritating and unnerving. She didn't like the feeling. Why was she the centre of his attention?

The fireball moved into her line of sight. It hovered in front of her and swung from side to side as she tried to look past it at the shade. She stopped moving. The ball of light drifted to her left.

'This way please, Miss Blue,' it said insistently.

She didn't move and stared impassively at the mini sun. Then she snapped. 'Will you stop calling me that! My name is Thistle!'

The fireball glowed brighter but there was no verbal response.

Her emotions were in turmoil. Once again, the disturbing image of Nan's corpse flashed before her eyes. There was a simmering rage and deep sorrow. Somehow she had to let it out, to vent it all. She felt the stare from the shade across the road. Enough was enough. She would confront him. One shade was enough and she sensed, now she had been spotted, that this one was going to follow her if she didn't take action. She would tell him to shove off. She would tell him to go bother someone else. There were plenty of other witches out there. Maybe she could refer him to someone else, if that was possible.

She thought about consulting her promptuary. She could ask for help. Maybe The Organisation had some answers. In any case, she had to get rid of him. She thought it best if she did it herself. She would have to start doing this kind of thing at some stage. Now was as good a moment as any. Anaïs tried to calm herself. She didn't want to blow the situation out of proportion. It was just an irritating shade.

Out of the corner of her eye, she looked across the street. He was still there. She sighed and turned her head to meet his gaze. He held it and didn't drop his eyes, which exuded unnerving anger. Something disturbing was going on behind those thick glasses.

She looked both ways for traffic and, with a determined stride, crossed the street towards him. Prince followed like a dutiful dog. On the other side she stopped, put her hands on her hips and looked up at him. He wasn't as tall as she had expected. Strangely, his aura had made him seem bigger. He was still a lot taller than her, though. Everyone was.

Sternly, he looked down at her and took a piece of white chalk from the inside pocket of his jacket. He knelt and brought himself down to her level and uncomfortably close to her face. If he had been able to exhale, she would have felt his breath. Once more, he looked her square in the eyes. She looked away. He was invading her personal space and she took a step back.

He leant forward and placed one hand on the ground in front of him. In neat block letters he began writing on the footpath. The shopping crowd whirled around them, unconcerned by what he was doing. In the middle of the throng, Anaïs felt as if they were in an invisible bubble. She shut out her surroundings and concentrated on the shade.

The absence of a shadow made him seem to float above the ground, with the piece of chalk the only thing connecting him to it. He worked meticulously on each letter as if it were a work of art. Even with the chalk, his handwriting was refined. He finished writing and dropped the chalk back into his pocket. He wiped white chalk dust down one leg and stood up to appraise his handiwork.

On the footpath between them was scrawled a single word: *Julia*.

He questioned her with his eyes. Anaïs was unmoved.

'I can't help you,' she said.

The pain of disappointment in his eyes swiftly turned to anger. He stepped toward her. He looked desperate. She felt a hand on her shoulder. It was Prince. He gently spun her around.

'We should leave.'

She gave him a grateful smile and nodded. Prince looked at the shade and shot him a warning glare. The shade made a move towards them and then decided against it. He held his ground, unsure of himself, before letting his arms drop loosely at his sides in submission. He made no further attempt to approach.

Prince led her away. Anaïs felt sorry for the shade but his aggressive nature worried her. She glanced back over her shoulder as they walked away. The shade watched them leave. The letters flashed in white starkness at his feet. Within seconds the crowd closed in around him, obscuring both him and the scrawl on the pavement. The last thing she saw was his eyes smouldering behind the thick layer of glass.

THE BIG HOUSE

'You can't bring him in here,' said the woman at the door.

'I have no alternative,' replied Anaïs.

The woman glared down at her. 'Fiddlesticks. There are always alternatives.'

Anaïs and Prince had continued to follow the little sun through the streets. It had guided them to the front door of a majestic house in the centre of Amsterdam's Museum Square. Although she had often been in the area, she had not noticed the house before. It struck her as a strange place for such an expansive mansion. It was huge. It looked more like a cross between a palace and a castle than a house. It had turrets and cone-shaped roofs. It looked as though the original core of the building had been added onto without any thought to its outward appearance. Rooms jutted out irregularly from its sides and it was several storeys high. Some of its walls were flat, some were rounded. The building seemed to have a life of its own. Although she couldn't detect any movement in the walls of the house, Anaïs wondered if she was in danger by being so close to it.

Extending out from the centre of the building was a wide, stone staircase. It wasn't exactly inviting but it did make it clear where the entrance to the strange house was. Together, she and Prince had climbed the stairs. Upon reaching the upper landing the heavy, oak front door had swung open on well-oiled hinges. They had been expected.

'I can't leave him out here,' protested Anaïs.

The woman standing in the doorway was thin and bespectacled. She was unmoved by Anaïs's pleas. Her entire body was sharp-edged. She was smartly dressed in a business suit and her long, red hair was bundled up on her head like a crown. Anaïs's eyes dropped to her shoes. They were high-heeled and bright purple. Anaïs was jealous. Pinned to the lapel of her suit was a badge with the word 'librarian' printed neatly on it in elaborate lettering.

Anaïs tried to look past the woman and into the house, but couldn't see anything to suggest they were at the entrance to a library. She had a job title, that was clear. Maybe it was her responsibility to take care of a private book collection hidden in the depths of the mansion. The fact that the librarian knew what Prince was gave Anaïs the impression that perhaps she was a witch. However, there was no threat of a storm and the sky was clear, so perhaps not.

The librarian stood her ground and stared down her

nose at Anaïs. 'Of course you can leave him out here. It's not like he's going to run away. They don't do that if they have snagged one of you.'

One of you? This reinforced Anaïs's doubt about the librarian's witch pedigree. Anaïs creased her brow. 'What do you mean?'

'Exactly what I just said. He needs you more than you need him. It stands to reason he won't leave you,' said the librarian matter-of-factly.

'Oh, I wasn't afraid of that. He's my friend.'

The woman in the doorway smirked. 'They can't be friends.'

Anaïs was insulted and puffed out her chest. 'Well, he *is* my friend and he's coming in with me.'

She looked them up and down and let out a weary sigh. 'Fine. He can wait in the hall.'

Anaïs decided not to push her luck any further and accepted the offer. The librarian took a step back and held the door open, allowing them to pass. The ball of light, which had been hovering between them, shot into the house and disappeared. Anaïs jumped at the sudden movement. She hesitated.

The librarian remained unruffled by the light, but was clearly irritated by the little witch's lack of movement. She spat out her words. 'Hurry up! I don't want to stand here all day. It's freezing.'

Cautiously, Anaïs and Prince stepped through the small entranceway and proceeded into the spacious central hall of the house. Its high ceiling was intricately decorated. An enormous chandelier hung from the centre of a large ceiling rose. The ceiling and walls were covered with dark wooden panelling, etched with delicate carvings. A broad staircase swept up one wall like the curve of a swallow's wing. Perched on the leading edge of the bannister was a silver-plated cat. It was seated in an upright position on its haunches with its tail drooped over its paws. It was moulded with such realistic detail that it looked as if it would spring down from its mounting at any moment. Anaïs had the feeling its eyes followed her as she walked across the room. The hall itself was sparsely furnished. Against one wall was a small side-table and a dark-leather, Chesterfield *chaise longue*. Apart from these furnishings the house appeared to be empty.

Prince walked over to the sofa and sat down. *'I'll see you when you're finished,'* he said.

Anaïs eyed him and frowned. All of a sudden, she had the feeling that everyone else knew what was going on except her. Prince didn't look at her but stared down at the sable-stained, wooden floorboards beneath his feet. She felt deserted and certainly didn't want to be left alone with the strange woman.

The librarian turned and walked towards the staircase. 'Excellent. Follow me,' she said.

Reluctantly Anaïs did as she was told. To her surprise the librarian didn't climb the staircase but went to a small door under it. She opened it and carefully stepped down a narrow set of dimly lit stairs. Her high heels clacked loudly on the steps and echoed back up at Anaïs. The hollow sound gave the impression they were entering a cave. With some trepidation Anaïs followed her into the bowels of the house. Before leaving the room she shot one last glance at Prince. He squinted slightly, smiling with his eyes. It didn't make her feel any better about leaving him behind.

A GLIMPSE

As Anaïs descended into the cellar, Prince settled back on the sofa and watched the door swing shut behind her. He was unperturbed. It didn't bother him that he may have competition for her attention. He knew that he came first. If nothing else, he was assured of being the next one to get assistance. That was, of course, if she came back.

The likelihood of her return troubled him. He felt it his duty to protect her. He might be next in line but if she wasn't around, then she wouldn't be able to help him. If something happened to her, it would put a stop to his goal. He had a problem he needed to solve and she was the woman for the job. He didn't expect to find another like her. Witches didn't grow on trees.

He thought about the shade with the glasses. It was strange that the spectacles were visible, even through his camouflage. Prince had caught a glimpse of the real him in a nearby window. He wondered who Julia was and felt a bit jealous. This shade had a name to work with. It was a good deal more than he had to go on, or was it? A name on its own was worthless, unless, of course, it was an especially rare one. But Julia? There must have been thousands of them in the world.

This thought made him feel better about the confrontation and he smiled to himself. The shade was no better off than he was. In fact, he had the distinct advantage. He had the help of a witch.

Where was she?

He went to get up and then it hit him, a flash of incredibly bright light. It temporarily blinded him and pinned him back in the Chesterfield. It took a few moments to regain his vision. He rubbed his eyes with his knuckles. He squinted. He was no longer in the hall. He was still sitting on a couch. There were also stairs and a table. Only, they were situated in a large living room. Gone was the wooden panelling and floorboards. Everything was kind of, well, fluffy. Deep, shag-pile carpet swallowed up his shoes. Brightly coloured throw rugs were everywhere. They were tossed across furniture and even hung from the walls. He couldn't imagine a more contrasting set of furnishings to the those of the big house.

A huge colour television, set in a heavy wooden cabinet, took pride of place in the centre of the room. Images flicked sporadically across the screen. Most were of men in uniform frantically running around. They appeared to be arguing a lot and there were regular images of them sparring face to face. The television emitted no sound, but music came from somewhere in the corner of the room. The song was familiar but he couldn't identify it.

He felt warmth. It ran down his spine and along the backs of his legs. It wasn't him. It was the couch which was warm. It was incredibly soft and moulded to his body, not hard and unyielding like the tough leather of the *chaise longue*. The feeling running along his back was strange. How long had it been since he had really physically felt anything? Too long. He settled back into the sofa and wiggled from side to side. He let himself sink deeply into it, bathing in the heat. It felt so good.

Four men walked into the room. They were all dressed in black suits. One by one they approached him and extended their hands to be shaken. He obliged them, offering his own hand. Their touch was strange. He really felt it. Even when Anaïs touched him, although he felt the pressure, it wasn't tangible. The warmth of their grip was palpable.

The last of the four men approached him and proffered his hand. He wore spectacles with extremely thick glass. It was him, the shade. Prince was aghast. Reluctantly he shook the shade's hand. His grip was firm and he held on a little too long.

The men sat down on either side of him. They didn't say very much and when they did he had difficulty understanding what they said. They spoke English with a very thick accent which he couldn't quite place. He strained to hear what they were saying.

The shade drawled at him, 'Why don't you cut records anymore?'

Prince didn't understand. Records? Did he mean

files or documents? Why would he want to chop them up? Before he could enquire what the shade meant a woman appeared at the top of the stairs. She was tiny and young, a teenager. Was she another witch like Anaïs? No, her face was familiar. It was the face he'd seen in his mind's eye. It was her, the one he had been looking for. No, wait, it wasn't. But she was very similar.

The shade laid a hand on his shoulder and everything turned white, and then black. A moment of silence. Then he realised his eyes were shut. He was in control again. He snapped his lids open. He shook his head and tried to work out where he was. He was alone in a big room. On a couch, an old leather sofa, a Chesterfield. Very different to the one he had just been sitting on. This one didn't give off heat. It was hard, cold and uninviting. He slid his hand across the smooth leather. He could touch but couldn't feel it. He felt numb. He was back.

What had he just seen? Where had he been? Who were the men? And the woman? Who was the shade? Too many questions.

A movement in the room caught his eye. He looked up and across the empty hall. The wide staircase filled half the room and curved up the opposite wall. The silver cat sitting on its bannister slowly turned its head away from him and towards the front door.

CAPUT MORTUUM

I t was entirely unexpected and unlike any space Anaïs had ever been in. If the exterior of the house had given the impression of a castle, then the subterranean part reinforced this.

A long, narrow, curved staircase had led them down into the sparsely lit cellar of the house. The cellar was huge and cavernous. She could only just see the floor of the house high above. Great brick pillars supported it. She estimated that it was suspended at least two storeys above her head. They crossed the empty cellar and through a small door. She was then led down a seemingly endless vaulted tunnel. Old festoon lighting hung from the centre of the curved-brick ceiling from hooks. It looped its way along the corridor and illuminated very little. It was little more than a guide rope hanging out of reach above their heads. She even had trouble seeing the librarian walking a few paces in front of her. She hurried to keep up with her for fear of losing the thin woman in the semi-darkness. There was no indication when the tunnel would end and, after several minutes of walking, she was surprised when it did. Upon reaching its end they went through a small archway and mounted another steep staircase.

The well-worn stone stairs went up and up. They spiralled in a tight circle with only enough room for a single person. A metal railing provided some support and followed the line of the stairs like a thin black snake. Eventually they were confronted with a door.

Out of breath, the librarian fumbled with a set of keys on a brass ring. Finding the one she was looking for, she inserted and turned it. She put her weight against the heavy door and it swung open with a creak. They stepped out into another large, dimly lit room. The door creak once more and slammed shut behind her.

Anaïs turned to look behind her, but saw no door, only a huge painting of a group of men in medieval dress. They posed in full regalia, brandishing swords and spears. The painting covered the entire wall and was at least five metres high. The only female portrayed in it was a small girl, not much older than herself. Anaïs stood face to face with her. The positioning of the now hidden door was clearly behind the child. Anaïs searched for a trace of it but could see no evidence of a door frame. The girl had a strange look on her face, almost fear, and she appeared to be attempting to run from something. She held what appeared to be a dead chicken in her hand. Anaïs followed her gaze. Her eyes were trained on another painting in the gloominess across the room.

The librarian tisked and prodded Anaïs. 'Don't dilly-dally,' she snapped.

Anaïs followed her obediently. They crossed the room and through an archway into another room. They then walked through countless corridors of artworks. The librarian marched with unwavering purpose in front of her. Without a word, she silently led the way and barely acknowledged Anaïs's presence. The thought crossed her mind that perhaps she should could just slip away. It wasn't really an option, though. She wouldn't know where to go. They traipsed through big rooms and small, all of them dimly lit except for the glow of modern halogen spotlights picking the paintings off the wall. She passed huge wall murals depicting sailing ships engaged in battle on the high seas. She saw armies on horseback tending to the wounded and accepting defeat. She saw biblical scenes of plagues and people gorging themselves on the bodies of others. Portraits of men and women in stiff, white collars and funny square hats looked down upon her. She giggled and poked her tongue out at them. They stared sternly back down at her.

Once in a while the librarian would impatiently growl at her to follow. 'Come on, hurry up child.'

'Yes, yes,' she replied, bemused by the librarian's ungainly walk on high heels and the loud clicking of her stilettos on the floor.

Eventually they stopped in front of a huge grandfather clock. It was ancient and towered over her. The librarian pulled a fob watch out of her suit pocket and compared the time on the clock face to her own.

Anaïs looked at the pendulum through a glass door on the clock. It ticked loudly as it swung from side to side. The librarian reached up and opened the glass cover over the clock face. The clock was very tall and required her to stretch full-length in order to access the little door. Anaïs smirked at how ungainly she looked, balanced precariously on her stilettos.

The librarian tapped the minute hand gently to the left before closing the little glass door and relaxing her body. Her suit jacket had ridden up on her and she tugged it back down by the flaps and straightened it. She took a long, gold chain from around her neck with a single small key attached to it. She bent forward and inserted it in the main door on the front of the clock. She grunted and pulled the door towards her. To Anaïs's surprise the entire front half of the clock, pendulum and all, swung open.

'Right this way,' she said and stepped into the clock. Anaïs took a deep breath and followed.

Another empty corridor confronted them. This one had bare walls and was devoid of paintings. It was strongly lit by a line of fluorescent tubes. They buzzed like flies above her. She narrowed her eyes and tried to force them to adjust quickly to the sudden bright light. At the other end of the corridor was a pair of glass doors. Together they walked down the corridor towards them. Anaïs heard the door behind her click shut. She looked back. The entire wall surrounding the door was made up of the cogs and dials and other innards of the grandfather clock. It was as if the wall was alive. It popped and ticked and whirred incessantly. The librarian hissed at her. 'Hurry up.'

She opened one of the glass doors and indicated that Anaïs should go first. With some hesitation, Anaïs stepped through the open door and found herself in a dark room. She took a few cautious steps into the room, following the line of light on the floor cast through the doorway behind her.

Suddenly, bright light filled the room and blinded her. She instinctively drew her forearm up to shelter her eyes. She peered out from under it but could only see a tiled floor covered in detailed mosaic.

A woman's warm voice in the same tone as the mini-sun spoke. 'Welcome, Miss Blue, I'm pleased you could come so soon. My name is Caput Mortuum.'

THE HIGH COURT

Slowly, Anaïs's eye's became accustomed to the light. She dropped her arm and surveyed the room. She looked up. The room was long and narrow and bright light streamed down from above. The light was swallowed up as it descended and barely illuminated the floor at her feet. Her eyes were drawn to its source.

A curved glass ceiling floated several storeys above her head. Its frosted panels appeared to be one enormous skylight. It looked as if the sun was shining directly from above. As she dropped her eyes she realised the light was artificial. At the far end of the room was a set of three tall, slender, arched windows. They bordered the ceiling and ran halfway down the wall. The real sun shone through them. By its yellow glow and angle she could see that it was now setting. It filtered through the window frames, casting long shadows across one wall.

Three metal balconies encircled the room. They

were supported by a series of skinny steel columns that ran the full length from floor to ceiling. A staircase with intricate latticework spiralled up one corner of the room and linked the balconies. Tiers of numbered shelves filled the space between each level. They were neatly packed with thousands of ancient books. The books steadily increased in size towards the lower shelves. Great heavy volumes lined the bottom shelves at ground level, making the already high ceiling seem even further away. Anaïs had the impression she was standing at the foot of a deep chasm. She felt incredibly small and exposed.

The floor was a huge, intricate mosaic. From where she stood it appeared as if a giant snake wound its way across the floor. It was like being in the middle of a snakes-and-ladders game. The shelved walls resembled ladders and she stood on the head of an enormous serpent. She feared at any minute that it would rise out of the floor and launch her into the air and across the room. She followed the curve of its body until she came to the tip of its tail. It terminated in the centre of the room and at the feet of a small woman. She was seated and appeared to be in her early twenties.

Anaïs cursed under her breath. The woman was dressed in a light blue uniform. It wasn't even a nice shade of blue, if that existed. It was one of those pale, clinical tones.

Why, of all things, did she have to wear that colour?

Caput Mortuum stood, pushed back her chair with a screech and stepped forward. Anaïs cringed at the sound, locked her jaw and sucked air between her teeth.

P J WHITTLESEA

Apart from Caput Mortuum there were six other women standing on either side of her in a semi-circle. They varied in age but all wore the same uniform. Anaïs tried to ignore the uniforms and focussed on their faces, each looking at her with accusatory eyes. Other than the eyes and the uniform they were all very different. There seemed to be a cross-section of the entire world standing before her. Each woman had a different ethnicity. Caput Mortuum appeared to be the youngest and wore a headscarf. The scarf was white and framed her face.

The uniforms were familiar but Anaïs couldn't quite place them. *Perhaps they were nurses or even from some obscure monastery.* She discarded the nun idea as not all the women were wearing headgear. The wall of blue cloth and their stern faces made Anaïs uncomfortable.

Caput Mortuum attempted to speak but barely a sound escaped her lips. Her voice wavered and it looked as if she would collapse at any moment.

'I ... I,' she stammered and began to weep.

Anaïs was confused. Caput Mortuum's knees gave way and she sank almost all the way to the floor before being caught by the women on either side of her. They guided her back into her chair. One of them turned to Anaïs. Her eyes were piercing.

'We are very disappointed in you,' she said.

Anaïs was irritated. 'Why?'

The woman chose to ignore her question and continued, 'You have caused us a great deal of pain and bother.'

Anaïs didn't like the way she was being talked to. She began to simmer but kept silent.

'You have been called before this committee to answer for your actions.'

'Committee?'

'Yes, we represent The World Witch Organisation.'

Anaïs was shocked and surprised. This was her first direct contact with The Organisation. Everything she knew about them, she had heard from Nan, or through messages in her promptuary. She never expected that they would convene in Amsterdam, let alone get together at all. She didn't think it was possible for witches to safely be in such close proximity to one another.

She took a deep breath and tried to maintain her composure. 'What have I done?'

Caput Mortuum screamed at her, 'You killed my daughter!'

She slid to the floor and howled like a wounded dog. Her cry reverberated off the glass ceiling but was immediately extinguished by the mountain of books lining the walls. She cupped her face in her hands, her shoulders shuddering as she sobbed.

Anaïs screwed up her face. *Did she mean Nan? So, this was her mother? Nan's death wasn't her fault!* She dropped her guard and protested, 'I didn't kill anyone. There was an accident.'

'There may well have been an accident but you were the cause of it,' said one of the women standing on the edge of the circle.

Another one piped up in an accusing tone. 'You summoned someone.'

Anaïs retorted defensively, 'I did no such thing!'

She was frustrated. She needed more information and they weren't providing it. And then there was Caput Mortuum's pitiful display.

Nan had said very few good things about her mother. The pair of them had barely communicated. Anaïs felt that she had more right to mourn the death of her caretaker than anyone else. They had been inseparable. They had been the more genuine version of mother and daughter. Not this woman curled up on the floor, crying in Anaïs's opinion what amounted to crocodile tears. She looked down at the crumpled, sobbing mess and felt an anger growing inside her.

Anaïs stepped forward and barked at her. 'How dare you lecture me! I knew your daughter better than you. Where have you been all this time? Certainly not with her. She told me about you. You were never there. You're just like my own mother.'

One of the women standing over Caput Mortuum intervened. 'That's enough!'

She stepped between the two of them and glared at Anaïs. 'Don't think that you are the only one. We are all alone in this world, Anaïs. It is our lot.'

This set off the other women and the group erupted into loud discussion. Anaïs gritted her teeth and stood her ground.

The woman on the edge of the circle moved between them. She spread her palms and gesticulated towards the floor, motioning for calm. 'I think we all need to settle down.' She looked around the group and then down at Anaïs. 'You are not on trial here, Anaïs. We are only trying to work out what happened. Unfortunately, emotions are running high and that makes it all the more difficult.'

Anaïs pursed her lips. 'Then tell me what's going on.'

'That's the whole problem. We don't know for sure. We asked you here in the hope that you could provide us with some information. Then we will investigate further.' She paused and softened her tone. 'My name is Sojourner Pink and I will be heading up the investigation. Please tell me what you know, Anaïs.'

Anaïs grinned and wiped the smile quickly off her face when she realised it was inappropriate. *What a great name.* She took an instant liking to the woman.

'I don't know a lot really. At least, not why this all happened. A strange woman rang the doorbell. She barged into the house and grabbed me. Then there was an explosion and I was thrown clear. When the dust settled, the woman was gone, Nan was dead, and you called me to come here.'

Sojourner Pink considered this for a moment. 'Have you seen this woman before?'

'No.' Anaïs stopped and ran the events through her head. 'Well actually, yes, she was standing outside our house a few moments before she came in.'

'What was she doing?'

'Nothing in particular. She just stood there.'

'And before that?'

'Nan and I had just been shopping. I met a shade.' Anaïs paused. 'Shouldn't you be writing this down or something?'

Sojourner Pink shook her head and smiled at Anaïs. 'No, my promptuary has a photographic memory.'

'Oh?' Anaïs looked her over but couldn't see any tell-tale book-shaped lumps. Sojourner Pink's uniform snuggly hugged her body.

She continued, 'Do you think this shade and the woman are connected?'

'I don't think so, although now you say it, it could be possible.' Anaïs thought back to their meeting and discounted the idea. 'No, he was just standing alone outside the KFC. I approached him and not the other way around.'

'Why did you do that?'

Anaïs raised her eyebrows. 'Approach him?'

Sojourner Pink nodded.

'I don't know. He looked sad. I was worried he would attract attention to himself. I thought a natural might spot him and I felt I should help. That's our job, isn't it? I thought maybe then he would go away.'

'And then?'

'He was quite nice. I found out I could talk to him. He heard me and talked back. Well, it was more like he thought back. He's my first shade. I don't know. Is this normal?'

'I wouldn't call it normal. It all depends on the strength of the connection. I think you've been very fortunate for a first-timer. They are not always so communicative.' Sojourner Pink gave her a smile of encouragement. 'Congratulations on making your first coupling.'

Anaïs smiled back up at her. 'Thanks.'

Sojourner Pink turned to the others. 'I don't think we can go any further here. I have enough to start with and will have to do some investigating at the scene.'

The other witches nodded in unison. Caput Mortuum had stopped sobbing. She dusted herself off, stood and breathed in deeply. She straightened the front of her uniform and looked warily at Anaïs.

She measured her words. 'Anaïs, you may go. We have a lot to discuss here. Go back to your shade and see what you can do for him. We will call you in due course.'

'But—' Anaïs was at a loss as to what to do. She remained where she was.

Sojourner Pink cleared her throat. 'It's ok, Anaïs, we will talk later. You can go. I will send you a message through your promptuary if I need any information.' She gestured towards the glass doors. 'The librarian will see you out.'

Anaïs nodded and reluctantly padded to the exit. Troubled, she kept her head down and didn't look back.

The Organisation silently watched her leave.

THE CLEANERS

T he door closed softly behind Anaïs.

'She is very rebellious,' said Sojourner Pink.

'Yes, but so were you.' Isabelle Zuylan eyed her and held a finger to her lips. She paced over to the door, cracked it open and peeked outside. Satisfied that Anaïs was gone she closed the door and turned to the rest of the group.

'She will need a new caretaker,' she said.

'She has the shade,' said Agnes Imelie.

'That will never do,' said Isabelle. 'We need another natural.'

Caput stood and spat out her words. 'I don't have another daughter to sacrifice!'

'We are fully aware of that,' said Sojourner Pink, motioning again with her hands in an attempt to calm the upset witch. 'Your loss is also our loss.'

Caput was fuming. Anger now overrode sorrow. She puffed, 'Loss? Hang your loss! I want to know what caused this! I have lost a daughter here! You are all so calculating and dry. Where is the sympathy?'

'We are fully aware of your pain, Caput,' said Agnes. 'It's important we find out what she did. We haven't dealt very well with her. We have shut her out. She will never come clean about it this way. We need to get her on side and find the cause of all this. There are destructive forces at play here.'

'I agree,' said Sojourner. 'We must solve this post-haste.'

She turned to Caput. 'I'm terribly sorry about your daughter. We all are. Unfortunately, getting angry with Anaïs won't help. She is still a child. She has not yet gained full control over her powers. If we force her out on her own she will cause more damage. We need her to understand why it is so important we know what happened. We are all at risk here. Because of her actions they will know about this. They may even know about her. If they find her they will be able to track us.'

Restlessly, Isabelle wrung her hands. 'Right now we can do nothing more in these bodies. We must consult our promptuaries and reconvene as soon as possible. We must find a candidate to protect her. Let's start with that and deal with the rest afterwards. Sojourner, you can continue your investigation in Amsterdam. Are you close?'

'I am already on my way,' said Sojourner Pink.

'Good,' said Isabelle. 'The rest of us will deal with finding a new caretaker. Is twelve hours enough time for everybody?'

She looked around the group and they all nodded except for Caput Mortuum. She sniffed.

'Caput,' said Sojourner Pink, 'we will get to the bottom of this but we need your help.'

'Very well,' she replied. 'I just need time to come to terms with this.'

'We fully understand. Take your time. You know we are there for you,' said Sojourner Pink.

'Ok, then, it's settled,' said Isabelle. 'Peace be with you all.'

One by one the women's bodies shook as if a chill had run up their spines. The cleaners stood facing each other in a tight semi-circle. All of them were perplexed.

One of them spoke up. 'Were we finished in here?'

There was a long pause before another answered hesitantly, 'You know, I honestly don't remember if we even started in here.'

They looked around the room and then at each other. One of the women looked down at the front of her uniform and noted that it was wet. The woman standing next to her peered at her face which was framed in a headscarf. 'Are you all right? You look terrible. Have you been crying?'

The woman in the headscarf shook her head. 'No,' she said.

She pulled a compact out of her pocket and examined her face. Her make-up had run and left black streaks on her cheeks. 'Strange,' she said.

'Maybe you better go clean yourself up,' said her neighbour.

'Yes.'

On the edge of the circle one of the women said impatiently, 'I think it looks fine in here. Let's hurry up and do the rest. I want get out of here before midnight.'

The others nodded in agreement. The circle broke and they hurriedly dispersed, picking up their cleaning equipment at the door on the way out.

A lone chair looked as if it had been discarded thoughtlessly in the middle of the room. The last of the day's long shadows played over the bookshelves. There was no trace of The Organisation.

ORGANISING A MEETING

One problem The Organisation had was that it could never convene in one place. The other was that a certain amount of participation was required on the part of mere mortals.

If a group of people need to get together to discuss something, it is far better if they can do it face to face. Individuals can look each other in the eye and make decisions more quickly. A point of view or message is less likely to get garbled. Everything is more direct. In order to facilitate this method of meeting together, and avoiding the problems associated with too much power crammed into one space, a solution was needed. The answer to The Organisation's problem involved the use of naturals.

Possession is a complicated process. The possessed need to maintain a form of dual existence. The actual body, the shell, must become a vessel and the owners mind needs to be sent into a dormant state. It is fortunate that the human brain is so complicated and only a small percentage of it is actually used. This leaves an incredible amount of cerebral power for other purposes. There is more than enough room inside someone's head to accommodate multiple personalities. Fully fledged witches make use of this, particularly the members of The Organisation.

Getting people to assemble for a meeting is a logistical nightmare, even for naturals. With The Organisation this is especially complex. To start with, each member has to find a willing host. Not everyone will let you take over their body. Preferably, you need someone with a malleable mind.

For example, you could think along the lines of blonde people. Of course, this is a generalisation, and I don't want to go around insulting people, but you get the picture. A nuclear physicist is never going to let you in. Being stuck in their head is also no party. Whereas with the perceived misrepresentation of blonde people, the party invariably never stops.

If you are going to possess someone you need their full co-operation and you don't need your own attention diverted by a constant stream of equations running through the middle of everything. Someone who is quite content with staring blankly at the sky is preferred.

During possession you cannot take over someone's mind completely. The basics still need to function, otherwise you risk killing them, and that would defeat the purpose of the whole exercise. The host's brain still needs to command their vital organs. Thankfully, most of these sensors reside in one hemisphere, so you can take over the other one for your own personal use.

There are inconsistencies with how brains are used and, depending on the individual, rogue thoughts can further complicate matters—especially if they are flitting from one hemisphere to another. Possession is a fine balancing act and you need to have your wits about you.

Having found a body that will do the job, and one that allows you to do yours, solves only half the problem. There is still the conundrum of getting your host to the meeting. Under usual circumstances, possession requires that you are physically fairly close to your target. With the world's population hovering around the eight billion mark, there is an incredible amount of mental activity going on. If you are too far from your subject, you run the risk of having a bad connection or, even worse, of getting your wires crossed.

Since the advent of long-haul air travel the entire process has been made a lot simpler. Individual members can live practically anywhere. Back when transportation was not as efficient, members of The Organisation were forced to live on the outskirts of civilisation, at what was considered a safe distance. As a result, they were a lot less aware of what was happening in the rest of the world. All this has changed and they now have a better overview of the entire planet. Since the invention of flight they have also been afforded the relative luxury of freely choosing their respective domiciles. In terms of hosts, the only real prerequisite is having someone who can easily get time off work to travel halfway around the globe. Quite often flight attendants are enlisted for this task.

In crisis situations, however, there is not the time to

assemble in preferred bodies. The next best thing has always been to use cleaners. It's not an ideal solution, as most cleaners are much more intelligent than they are given credit for. However, the mundane act of cleaning itself induces a state of mental activity which is quite conducive to possession.

Every country has cleaners. Enough of them gather in one place, and usually where the general public doesn't see them. This makes them ideal candidates and The Organisation takes full advantage of this. At strategic points around the earth, cleaning crews are overseen by one of The Organisation's representatives. They ensure that, in an emergency, The Organisation can gather at a moment's notice.

FIREWORKS

All hell was breaking loose. As fast as the sun set, so did the growth in the number of detonations. The entire city was exploding. This had certainly made what had happened at Anaïs's house less out of the ordinary. Older houses in Amsterdam were also prone to gas leaks. There were plenty of explanations for why such an event could occur. The timing of it happening on this particular day was fortunate.

The city shook and vibrated with a barrage of pops, bangs and thuds. The occasional deep whump of a particularly large firework sounded in the distance. If there was ever a night to be walking the streets undisturbed with the dead, this was it. The city had swelled by the tens of thousands with visitors, and the shade community took to the streets with them.

As Anaïs and Prince walked down the steps of the big house they were confronted with smoke and flashes of light and ear-splitting noise. The cacophony grew with every step. Anaïs looked across the grassed square and up at a section of glass-topped roof on the Rijksmuseum. She realised it was where she had just been. Slowly, some of the mysteries were becoming less so. She took stock of her surroundings.

The acrid smell of sulphur bit at her nostrils. It left a bitter taste in her mouth and forced tears to her eyes. She held them back. She didn't want to cry. She had done enough of that. She would be strong. The wind blew smoke in her face and one tear escaped. She squinted and it ran down alongside her nose and made an effort to reach her mouth. She brushed it aside before it got there.

As dusk descended, the museum was occasionally lit by the flashes in the sky around it. Its gothic spires looked particularly menacing in the light. They cast momentary shadows at different angles across the ground at her feet. She shrank back from them and up against Prince. She wasn't ready to be strong on her own. Even though the shade's touch was icy, it provided the warmth of companionship she desperately needed.

He sensed her trepidation and put his arm around her, pulling her close.

It had all been too much for her. She didn't want the responsibilities that had been cast on her shoulders. She just wanted time to grow up like everyone else. She couldn't. She was in the spotlight. Now that she was exposed and had attracted attention to herself, she could no longer play at being a witch. She had to do it for real. She couldn't fall back on her caretaker. Nan wasn't there to protect her anymore. Because of Nan's connection, and her mother being of such importance to The Organisation, Anaïs also couldn't hope to have much support from the upper levels of witchdom. She hadn't exactly made an enemy of them, but it would take time for them to forgive what they perceived were her actions. If it were solely up to Caput Mortuum, it might take forever.

Time heals all wounds, so they say, even supernatural ones. Only, witches have exceedingly long lives and correspondingly long memories.

A wave of sadness swept over her. The image of Nan lying in the rubble pushed all other thoughts aside. She still hadn't had the opportunity to fully come to terms with her death. Anaïs nestled her head deeper into the crook of Prince's arm. She let the tears flow. She sniffed and snorted.

Prince stood stock still. He froze. He didn't know what to do. The touch of another body caused turmoil. It confused him. It had been such a long time since something like this had occurred. Human touch was a completely new sensation to him in his new form. He knew he should console her with words but he didn't know what to say. He was glad that there was some form of physical contact, even if it unsettled him. Otherwise he would have felt completely useless.

She wiped her wet face on her sleeve and mentally tried to straighten herself out. It was time for action. Organisation or no Organisation, she had to do something about her situation. She had to find out who the strange witch was, or determine if she was indeed a witch. She had to find out why the woman had risked so much to get close to her. What was it that she had to communicate in person that couldn't be done using a host? And what had Anaïs done that had been so wrong? There was the name thing, but why was that so important?

Anaïs wasn't sure of her next move. Not specifically knowing the crime made it difficult to rectify any wrongdoing. How do you fix something when you don't know what you've broken?

She decided to concentrate on finding out what exactly she had done. She pulled her promptuary out of her coat and spoke into it. 'What have I done wrong?'

'You will have to be more specific,' said the promptuary.

Anaïs had to think. 'What caused the explosion at my house?'

'You came too close to another witch.'

Anaïs pursed her lips. 'Why was she there?'

'You have stolen her name,' replied the promptuary.

'Oh.' *So it was the name.* 'How do I give it back?'

'With great difficulty.'

Exasperated, Anaïs growled at the book, 'You're not very helpful.'

'Indeed, you are correct. I am a promptuary. My name is not Very Helpful.'

Anaïs pulled a face. 'You are also not very funny.'

'That may be so, but that is your opinion and I don't have opinions.'

Anaïs slammed the book shut and stuffed it back into her pocket. This wasn't getting her anywhere. Why did the promptuary even have a personality? And an irritating one at that.

Prince still held her loosely in his embrace. This further irritated Anaïs. She recoiled and ducked out from under his comforting arms.

'Get away from me!' she yelled at him.

She felt restricted. She didn't want the responsibility of having to deal with him anymore. It was enough coping with her own situation without the added burden of him. He was overbearing, or at least that was how she began to perceive him.

What did he want? Why was he hanging around her anyway? She couldn't help him. She didn't know where to start. It was all beyond her. She didn't really even want to help him. She had her own problems. Let him deal with his own lot. Let him find someone else. Right now it was more than she could handle.

He reached out to her and she stepped back even further.

'Don't,' she said. 'Just leave me alone.'

He shot her a hurt look. She ignored him and turned her back to him. She could feel him still hanging there on her shoulder. It was as if he was leaning on her. She felt pressured. Hemmed in. She couldn't breathe. Her stomach churned. The air caught in her throat and she sensed the bile rising. Why didn't he move? Why was he still here? She blocked the urge to throw up. She gritted her teeth and breathed out softly through her nose. She closed her eyes and listened to the sound of her own breath. A moment of calm. Then she snapped, spun around and flashed her eyes at him.

'Enough!' She pushed him away. 'Look, I can't handle this. You have to leave. Go find someone else to help you.'

She spun on the spot, turning her back to him, and stamped away across the grass. She shot a glance over her shoulder. He'd gotten the message and wasn't following.

Good.

It would be best to get as far away from him as possible, and then she could clear her head. Maybe none of this would have happened if he hadn't been around. In fact, she thought, everything had been fine before he turned up. So, it must have something to do with him. He was the cause of all this. If he wasn't around, then perhaps everything would return to normal. Perhaps. But it couldn't go back to normal, not anymore. Nan was gone.

She began to sob uncontrollably. What was going on? What was happening to her? All of this was too much. She needed time to think. But she couldn't think. Her head was swimming, not only with the thoughts running rampant in her head. There was noise everywhere, getting louder by the minute. Why? Where was it coming from? Everywhere, it seemed. What on earth was happening? Then she remembered.

It was New Year's Eve.

A VOYEUR

He couldn't be sure if she was one. It was just a feeling.

He had watched her march away from the old man. She was clearly upset. There was a purpose in her stride that gave her away. Five-year-olds don't walk with such purpose. They don't have goals. They are not so focussed. In general, they do what they're told. They don't make decisions the way she'd just done, and an old man, presumably her grandfather, would certainly not let her go like that. Something else was going on.

The hound growled at his side.

'Settle,' he murmured through his teeth.

The dog was so tall he could lay his hand on its back without bending down, and he was not a small man. The animal sniffed the air and looked up at him. The red glow of its eyes unnerved him. It stepped forward, tugging in earnest at its invisible leash. He clenched his fist more tightly around the short, thick, heavy chain that controlled the beast. The links in it snapped taut, wrenching at his arm and forming a u-shape around his hand. He widened his stance and leant his full weight against it. The trailing ends of the chain levitated in mid-air, almost horizontal to the ground and in line with his arm. They followed the movement of the dog and traced a line directly to its great head.

He wasn't entirely certain he could control the animal if it decided to take off. The problem didn't lie with the dog itself. It was trained to obey him. He did not have sufficient confidence in his own abilities, and watching the muscles ripple across the hound's shoulder blades, he doubted his own strength. His training had been extensive, but nothing beat real world experience. This was something he sorely lacked.

He hated the smell of the beast and pulled his nose away from it. The stench was like a stale fireplace that badly needed cleaning. The ash had stopped smouldering long ago, yet it still gave off its bitter odour. Even the act of laying a hand on the hound stirred up more fumes. It irritated him so much he had taken to smoking a cigar. The sweet smoke was the only thing that had been reasonably successful in covering up the reek of the dog.

The hound strained again, following the scent it had picked up. As the animal yanked at its leash, the ends of the chain whipped from side to side. He felt it jerk violently at his shoulder, threatening to rip his arm out of its socket. He held his ground, solidifying his stance. He made a similar mental adjustment, reassuring himself that he was in control. He pulled the chain close to his body and stepped up to the dog's flank. His leg brushed its fur and raised more of the putrid odour. He held the animal back with a wave of his free hand in front of its snout.

'Steady,' he commanded.

The beast whined and reluctantly obeyed, sitting back on its haunches. Its nostrils flared as it continued to sniff the air. The scent wasn't coming from the child alone. The dog wasn't the only one with a heightened sense of awareness. He sensed there was someone else. It was more than a hunch. He wasn't the only one following her. This made him unsure of his true goal. Somewhere nearby, there was another, more powerful entity. He feared it may not be something the beast could ward off. He may even need assistance, but he couldn't call on any right now. He was on his own.

He had been scrambled into action with no notice. Something tremendous was afoot. The Brotherhood's directive was simple: investigate the strange happenings in the city. Although he had been closest to the incident, he was unfamiliar with the lay of the land and was forced to rely heavily on the beast. He had eyes and ears but not its sense of smell. It could sense the other world.

Together they stood at the entrance to one of the arched tunnels leading from under the Rijksmuseum. He noted the scorch marks left by the hound's paws on the stonework. They would disappear by themselves, eventually. If at all possible, however, they must avoid leaving any trace of their presence. If someone were indeed tracking them, and in their vicinity, they would have no problem following their path.

He shifted his focus back to the child. She was storming off across the grassy square and into the distance. He watched as the old man judged that he had given her enough headway and set off after her. The Inquisitor decided to follow them. If there really was someone else on their trail then he hoped who, or whatever, it was would reveal itself to him. The child could serve as bait. She was important. That was all he knew and it was enough. He had little alternative.

The Inquisitor and the hound began to follow Anaïs and Prince. As they walked away from the building a figure in black with a wide brimmed hat stepped out of the folds of the masonry. It watched them go. In turn it followed as well.

A MAN AND HIS DOG

Anaïs had to do something. She couldn't continue to wander the streets. She was tired and drained. All she wanted was to go back to bed. If she slept on it, maybe things would be different when she woke. The problem was that she had no bed. She had nowhere to go. She was homeless.

The Organisation had cut her off. She could go back on her hands and knees and ask them to take her in. She doubted they would do that. She had done too much damage and it would take time before she could ask for sympathy. For the moment, she was on her own. It was up to her to sort it all out.

She thought about Prince. Maybe she had been wrong to desert him. He hadn't done anything but stand by her. And right now, she had no one else. He was it. He was all she had. Perhaps it was in her best interest to help him. He certainly needed her. He hadn't been pushy as she had been. He hadn't demanded things. Maybe she should try to be more like him. Maybe they were right. Maybe she should help him.

She leant back against the leading edge of a park bench and looked across the square. Night had now completely descended but it was not dark. Fireworks continued to light up the sky. The noise of a city in flames continued unabated around her. She climbed up onto the bench and sat down. She slid herself back and nestled her spine against the backrest. Her feet dangled over the edge, not reaching the ground. She let her head rest on the wooden slats and looked up. She watched the sky above her explode.

From her perch she commanded a complete view of the square. There were people everywhere. Small pockets of revellers were drinking and yelling at each other, trying to hear each other above the din. A single rogue rocket screamed from one side of the square to the other at about one metre off the ground. Somehow it negotiated its way between the groups of revellers without making contact. She watched with bemusement as those who saw it coming jumped or dived out of its trajectory. It crashed harmlessly into the unrelenting wall of the museum. A moment later its contents exploded. The noise was deafening. Its percussive boom slapped the ground. The sound resonated around the open square and bounced off the surrounding buildings. With the explosion, a great arc of bright blue sparks erupted from the crash site. It cast everyone between her and it in silhouette.

She smiled at the madness. And then the smile melted. Standing in the middle of the square, almost completely isolated from the throng, was a solitary figure. He hadn't flinched like the rest of the people. He was oblivious to what was going on around him. Even more disturbingly, the animal at his side was also seemingly unaware of the chaos around it. The animal was the biggest dog she had ever seen. Its withers were as broad as a bodybuilder's. Its long, bulky coat of fur fluffed out from its sides and seemed to defy gravity. Dogs have very keen senses, yet it seemed entirely unperturbed by the acrid smell and thunderous noise. She could have sworn that its eyes were piercing, red points of light. They shone out beneath the long fringe that draped over its snout.

A rocket burst above them. A burning ember suspended from a small parachute descended slowly and lit them up, enabling her to see the pair in more detail.

She studied the man. He was well built, broad shouldered. With his shaved head he came across as almost brutish. He wore a three-quarter-length coat which fit very snugly. It was wrapped tightly around his torso and fanned out at his knees. A pencil-thin, almost clerical white collar encircled his neck. Her eyes settled on his face and everything suddenly fell silent. Ataraxia prevailed. It was as if she was in a bubble.

The parachute descended further. The flare beneath it touched the ground beside the two figures, completely illuminating the man and dog.

His eyes were directed down at the beast. He seemed to be studying it carefully. She could now make out the details of his face. He was young, in his early twenties and possibly only a year or two older than her mental self. His features were fine and chiselled. His skin smooth and creaseless. There was a certain innocence about him. There was something serene about his countenance. He tilted his head to one side and looked up. Their eyes met. The innocence dissolved and melted away. He had old eyes. They had seen much more than his face implied. Serenity was instantly replaced with purpose. The bubble popped.

The sky above them roared with a fresh burst of shells. A rapid-fire clatter of deafening cracks. A fresh shower of New Year's ammunition rained down on the square. She clapped her hands to her ears.

The cacophony was like a starter's gun for the man and the dog. They leapt out of their blocks and launched themselves straight towards her. Her response was spontaneous, the danger more than apparent. She slid forward on the bench. Her legs still dangled in mid-air. Before her feet touched the ground someone whisked her up into their arms.

She had a last glimpse of the two figures running towards her. Something else swept behind them in a dark blur. The legs of the man and the dog were whipped out from under them. They both crashed to the ground, the man falling upon the dog in a tangle of arms, legs and tails.

And then her face was buried in a chest. It was a barrel of a chest. A man's chest. There was no soft bulge of a breast, only the sharp hardness of a sternum. A large hand held her head against it. It was cold. The hand firmly gripped the back of her small skull. She struggled to free herself. He was too strong. She relented and let her body go limp. She thought about her promptuary but couldn't reach it. Her arms were pinned between her own body and the chest. Held securely in a bear hug, there was no escape. Her captor wasn't going to let go.

She felt his heavy footfalls as he ran and the jarring as his heels hit the ground. They reverberated through his body. The blows were softer for her. She floated on gentle undulations. Up and down. She heard his laboured breathing. He puffed and grunted. But he wasn't breathing. It was merely air being expelled from his lungs every time his feet hit the ground. There was no heartbeat. Even with her ear pressed tightly to his breast so that it shut out all other sound, she heard no blood pumping. The comforting thump of a heart was missing.

She missed Nan. With Nan there would have been the warmth and comfort of the beat. But she was gone. Someone else held her tightly. Only the sound of air in dormant lungs emptying and filling with the exertion of his body. It creaked and groaned as if it hadn't been exercised for a long time.

It seemed as though he ran for an eternity. Sometimes she felt him pull to the left and then to the right as if he was dodging something. Occasionally she heard snippets of people talking and then nothing. He ran on. She felt him stumble and nearly fall. He regained his balance and then he slowed. She felt them radically change direction one last time and then they stopped.

He bent forward, released her from his vicelike grip

and set her down. He dropped to his knees, his face centimetres from hers. He held an index finger to his lips and implored silence with his eyes.

It was very dark but she could still make out his features. It was Prince.

HIDING

'Thank you,' she whispered.

'Don't mention it.'

He was panting heavily from the exertion of the run. She could hear it when his words sounded in her head.

Anaïs kept her voice low. 'Who were they?'

Prince was silent for a moment. She could sense him mulling it over.

'I don't know, but they didn't mean well.'

'I got that much.' Anaïs recalled the piercing eye contact she had made with the Inquisitor. 'Somehow, he knew me.'

She tried to read Prince's face but was only met with the stoic look of his camouflage.

'What are we going to do?' she asked.

'I have no idea. I didn't think that far ahead.' He laid a hand on her shoulder and a shiver ran up her spine from his cold touch. *'It might be a good idea to check if we were followed.'* Prince moved away from her and stood up. He

kept his voice low, even though no one else could possibly hear him. *'Stay here. I'll go look.'*

'Ok.' She knotted her brow. She didn't want to be left alone again. 'But don't be long.'

His eyes twinkled reassuringly. *'I won't.'*

Prince slid quietly along the wall next to them. The darkness swallowed him up. She looked around. They were in a very narrow alley. Above her was a thin sliver of sky, lit by the occasional firework. The sounds of the explosions were soft and distant. The alley was not only dark, it was also unusually quiet and in stark contrast to where they had just been. There was a streetlight at one end where the alley met a wider street. She watched as Prince appeared under it. He stuck his head around the corner. He then pulled it back and stared at the opposite wall for a moment. Again he peered around the corner, this time for longer. He turned and moved back down the alley to her. He knelt down beside her.

'I don't see anything, but I don't think it's a good idea to wander around out there.' He glanced over her shoulder towards the opposite end of the alley. *'Let's find a place to hide for the night. I would feel more comfortable moving in daylight.'*

Anaïs nodded grimly. 'I agree.'

'Stay here,' he commanded gently.

She dipped her head in affirmation. Prince slid along the wall again, this time in the other direction. There, with no streetlight to provide illumination, the darkness was absolute. She couldn't tell how far the alley went or whether it even terminated. She heard the tinkling of glass breaking and a door being forced.

There was a loud scraping and a creak. Moments later she heard him shuffling back towards her.

His face appeared out of the inky blackness centimetres from her own. She caught her breath in surprise.

Prince whispered in her ear. *'Let's go.'*

She let him take her hand. His cold grip sent a chill through her once again and she fought the urge to shiver.

A few metres down the alley was an open doorway. He guided her inside. Broken glass crunched under her feet. He closed the door softly behind them. She heard him drag a heavy piece of furniture across the floor. He fumbled around and then she heard a click. A single compact low energy light bulb hung from a strand of wire in the centre of the room. It grew steadily brighter until it illuminated the entire space, a small room.

She could now see the door. A small pane of glass next to the handle was missing. Shards of glass lay scattered on the floor. There was a small table near the door. The rest of the room was empty except for a two-seater couch and an office chair. They were in a small reception room. It appeared abandoned and disused. An old blanket lay on the couch.

She lay on the couch, pulled her knees up to her chest and curled into a tight ball. Prince drew the blanket over her up to her chin. He sat on the table near the door, reached over and flipped the light switch. It took some time for her eyes to adjust to the darkness. When they did she could just make out his silhouette in front of the glass door. Occasional flashes in the sky outside lit him up from behind.

She closed her eyes and soon fell asleep. She dreamt. Her dreams were filled with the vivid image of a giant, red-eyed dog running towards her. The image repeated itself over and over. Something blocked the dog from actually getting to her. She didn't feel fear, more a kind of fascination, until it eventually stopped trying to reach her. It was then that it opened its mouth and the fear flooded in. Between its razor-sharp teeth she saw that it had the forked tongue of a snake. It flicked menacingly at her. An iciness hit her and froze her entire skull. The dog wheezed and hissed in a deep tone.

'Anaïs?'

SLEEP

Prince watched her toss and turn on the couch. She was truly petite, a little ball of flesh curled up under the blanket. He wanted to hold her again. The embrace had felt good. Curiously, it felt familiar, holding a child so tightly in his arms. He sensed it was an experience he'd had before. Now that he had felt it again, he missed it. He wished he could place the source of the original feeling. It had come from being with someone else, someone very much like Anaïs. It made him think of her, the one. Could it be she was also lost and alone, maybe an orphan?

And what of Anaïs and her parents? Where were they? Surely somewhere out there a father existed, and a mother. Why had they deserted her? He didn't know enough. Maybe, if he knew more, he could help her find them, and then he would find what he was searching for.

He was still looking. He was always doing that. He searched his thoughts but the image of the one like Anaïs wouldn't come. Was it really a child he was looking for? Maybe he was wrong. He wasn't convinced. It was definitely a somebody, not a something. It was driving him mad. He patted his forehead with his fingertips. He knew the memory fragment was there somewhere. It was buried deeply, hidden away, but it was there.

Be patient, he told himself. *It will come.*

Anaïs cried out in her sleep, yelping like a puppy.

It snapped him out of his thoughts. Other, more serious concerns filtered into his head. He didn't like what was going on. It disturbed him. The man and the dog; had he seen them somewhere before? He couldn't be sure. How his memory tortured him! What were they after? Was it just her or something more? Now that he had helped her, had he also put himself at risk? What or who they wanted was immaterial; they were dangerous. He and Anaïs must not get caught.

If he had been alone it would have been easier to escape. He was used to staying under the radar. She was a new addition to the equation, a responsibility. She complicated his very existence.

Furthermore, he sensed she hadn't been in this position before, in real danger. They had kept her so well hidden. They had been clever. Now she was exposed and couldn't avoid detection as easily as before.

One thing was certain. The man and the dog were still out there somewhere looking for them. He and Anaïs no longer had freedom of movement. Not that it had really been the case before. But now they were the hunted. And the hunted need to hide. From now on, they would always be looking over their shoulders.

Anaïs stirred again on the couch. She grunted and kicked. The blanket slid to the floor.

He went to her and laid a hand gently on her forehead. There it was again. The familiarity. What was it? She shuddered under his touch. He withdrew his hand. Her face contorted. She kicked and tried to scream.

He softly spoke to her. *'Anaïs?'*

Her eyelids flipped open. Fear filled her eyes and plastered itself across her face. She looked straight through him. She was still deeply asleep. She stared long and hard. Her eyelids fluttered, and then she closed them and was silent. Her body relaxed and she sank back into the couch. Her breathing became slower and deeper. It regulated itself.

He drew the blanket back over her and left her, satisfied that the nightmare was over. He went back and sat on the table. For the rest of the night she slept soundly. He watched her and mulled over the strange sensation he had felt when they had touched. Who had made him feel the same way?

WHISPERS

Have you ever thought you heard someone calling your name? More than likely someone *was* calling your name. Perhaps it was a relative or friend passing by on the other side of the street. Or perhaps it was a stranger calling someone with the same name. Or possibly it was some other noise floating on the wind which emulated the sound of your name. More than likely it was none of these things. Maybe it was a shade.

Shades instinctively know the inner workings of the human mind. Many of them have spent an inordinate amount of time mulling over the stuff between their own two ears. Particularly if they have lived a long existence as one of the living. This knowledge is necessary if you wish to influence others. But having mountains of knowledge won't help you if you don't know how to use it.

Some shades have terrible memories of reality. The longer they are in a shadow state, the less they can recall from the real world. It is best if a shade can get out of their state of uncertainty as quickly as possible. Too much of the wrong knowledge can be detrimental, especially if then and now become muddled. They can become convinced of a false reality. After all, if you think you know it all, you're not going to be very open to working out what you should be doing. Sifting through memories requires an open mind.

Shades need help, but are capable of planting thoughts in other people's minds. Have you ever been busy doing something and then, out of nowhere, thought, *I should be doing that*? You drop what you're doing and follow the mental command. You feel obliged to do it.

Influence works on many levels. It's most successful when something is hinted. Influence doesn't work if it's too obvious. Subtlety is the name of the game. It's nearly impossible to convince someone to do something against their will if you broach the subject head-on. This is where practical knowledge plays an important role. Tact is something that can only be learnt with experience. You have to do it over and over until you find what works best. There are general rules but, apart from that, you will need an intimate knowledge of someone to get them to truly do something against their will.

The dead have the power to influence. They know exactly how to approach someone. Especially if that someone is a person they have dealt with in life. Through past experience they know when and what to say. Timing is as important as what is said. This is why the command 'Go do that now' works. Shades, who have an intimate knowledge of someone, can see their window of opportunity coming up. They know exactly when to jump in and send a command. They know when to manipulate. If a string of directives can be achieved you can almost guarantee having control over an event. It's not a simple thing and does require planning. A good deal of practise also does not go astray.

Anaïs and Prince were novices. They knew nothing. They had no inkling of the power that they possessed as a combined force. They were volatile weapons that could go off at any moment.

THE INQUISITOR

Where *was she? Not only that, who or what were the others?*

He suspected the old man was a shade. If so, then he had given himself away. That was a mistake. But then, maybe not. Shades were constantly changing appearance. They were hard to track. You could only catch them if they weren't aware of you and you still had the element of surprise.

He had lost that now. He didn't have the benefit of camouflage as they did. He had certain powers, but still had much to learn. He was still serving his apprenticeship.

The shade wasn't dangerous. At least, he didn't think so. If it gave itself away again he would know what to do. What concerned him more was the other one. Something had knocked him off his feet. It was strong, so powerful it had floored the dog. And the animal was not easily brought down.

The beast had its great head in his lap. The weight

of it was substantial, its skull solid and heavy like a lump of granite. The Inquisitor ran his fingers slowly through the deep fur around its neck, trying his best not to raise its stale smell. It growled softly, rumbling like distant thunder. He leant back on the bench, his spine cracking as he straightened it.

He watched the drunken party-goers carve unsteady paths across the square. It had been a long night and he was tired. He'd had enough of the festivities. Although, at one point, he had been tempted to join in, he had held his guard. He had a job to do. He had permitted himself one long, strong scotch. It had burnt a line of white heat down his gullet and warmed his belly. It had helped him get through the bitter cold which was growing as dawn approached. He wished he had another now.

The dog kept him warm. It was, after all, a hell hound. They were the best blanket ever invented. It looked up at him with its bloodshot eyes. He wondered if they mirrored his own. He needed sleep. He would permit himself an hour of rest and then he would continue the search.

He looked around the bench. She had sat here. Through the slats he checked if there was any evidence on the ground beneath it. There was nothing.

He sighed. He didn't have anything to go on. After some rest he would retrace his steps and fan out from the square. They had disappeared quickly. She couldn't be far away and had to be hiding close by. She was a child, small and fragile, and would need rest. He had the benefit of age and could stay active for longer. At this moment, though, he was exhausted. Now he had to rest as well. The dog would keep watch. He hoped a policeman wouldn't come and ask him to move on. That would wake him. However, he felt fairly certain he wouldn't be disturbed. It was New Year's Day and he wouldn't be the only one curled up on a park bench. The police would turn a blind eye to anyone not stirring up trouble. They had better things to do.

He had little choice. Without rest he would be useless. He closed his eyes and tried to clear his mind. An hour was all he needed and then he would be able to think clearly again. The dog was restless. He stroked its great head and let his own body relax. Even the pungent smell of cinders under his nostrils didn't bother him. He was too tired.

'Shh,' he said. The dog settled.

Good.

Soon she would be waking. Soon she would be on the move. Then they would be exposed. Then he would find them.

NEW YEAR'S DAY

Her eyes snapped open. She looked around the room, taking a moment to recall where she was. Prince was still sitting on the table. He stared blankly at the wall behind her. He hadn't moved and held exactly the same position as before she fell asleep.

Anaïs cleared her throat and barked at him light-heartedly. 'Hey!'

Her voice wrenched him out of his stupor. He shook his head to clear it. The sound of another voice directed straight at him was still new and at first took him by surprise. He dropped his eyes and looked down at her. He smiled, his words sounding in her head.

'Hey yourself!' he said.

Anaïs frowned. 'Have you been there all night?'

'Of course. I have nowhere else to go, do I?'

She pursed her lips. 'I wouldn't know about that.'

He shuffled uneasily on the table and looked at her

timidly. *'Even if I did, I'd still prefer to be here. I like being around you. You remind me of someone.'*

'Really?' She raised an eyebrow. 'Who?'

He sighed and wrung his hands. *'I don't know exactly, just somebody. I wish I knew who it was.'* He paused and cocked his head. *'I was kind of hoping you could help me.'*

'I don't see how I can really help.' Anaïs sat up on the couch and pulled the blanket snugly around her waist. 'I know nothing about you.'

Prince looked solemnly at the floor. *'Then we share the same problem. I also have no idea who I am.'*

'Don't you remember anything about yourself. I mean, before you died?'

He peered at her from under his lids and then dropped his eyes to the floor. *'Only little things. I think I remember my mother. She was quite a big woman. She was always around, even when I got older.'* He sniffed. *'I'm pretty sure I also had a brother. The odd thing is I can't remember his face or any details about him at all; almost as if he was never there.'* He drew a circle with his foot in the dust on the floor. *'One thing keeps coming back to me. I remember being blinded by lights, like I was being interrogated. Also, there seemed to be lots of people around me, always. I was never completely alone. And the people, they were yelling and screaming, making lots of noise.'* He paused, contemplating the memories *'Most of all, I remember the noise.'*

Anaïs caught a glimpse of the real him in his reflection in the window beside him. His hair was dark and wavy, his face fatter, and he looked a lot younger. She stood on the couch. There was a large mirror on the wall behind her.

She beckoned him to come over 'Can you come here for a minute?'

He nodded. *'Sure.'*

He slid off the table and padded across the room to her. She pulled him closer then turned to the mirror. She looked past her own reflection and over her shoulder at his face.

'You look different in the mirror,' she said.

'Really?'

'Yes. It's odd. Your reflection in the window is hazy.' She turned to face him. 'Your face is much clearer when I look at you in the mirror. In the window it ripples like a reflection in water.'

'That's interesting, but I wouldn't know. For me there's no difference. No matter where I look I see the same reflection.'

Anaïs turned once more to the mirror. 'Your face is familiar. I can't quite place it, though.' She scrutinised his reflection. 'You know, I think perhaps you were famous.'

'Ok.' Prince grinned. *'That's good. It should make it easier for us to work out who I am.'*

Anaïs shot him a serious look. 'Us?'

Prince looked at her worriedly. *'You are going to help me, aren't you?'*

Anaïs grinned and nudged him in the ribs. 'Of course I'll help you. I was only joking. You saved my skin, remember?'

Prince nodded grimly.

She squeezed his arm and a chill ran up her own. 'I'm sure that any notoriety you have will help us work out who you are. Unfortunately, it's not our only problem.'

Prince studied the look of concern on the little witch's face and his thoughts returned to the events of the previous evening. *'Yes, you're right. We have another, much bigger problem.'*

OUTSIDE

Prince stuck his head outside to check if the alley was empty. There was nobody. Only the sound of sporadic thuds: the occasional distant burst of a firework. The sun was creeping down the alley. It wasn't even really daylight yet. It was just the darkness receding. The black turning to grey.

They had to find another spot while it was still early. It would be best to keep moving until they found something suitable. Now that she had lost her hideout they needed another place of sanctuary. But where could they go? He felt useless. He was as lost as her and didn't know how to help. It wasn't necessary for him to have shelter like her. He was dead and didn't need a roof over his head. The thing that sheltered him, his disguise, moved around with him.

They slipped out into the alley and began walking. It was cold and she took the blanket with her, wrapping it tightly around her torso and over her head like a greatcoat. All the while he checked for other signs of life, looking around every corner before entering another street. The streets were deserted. Before long they stepped out onto a main road. Shredded paper, the torn wrappings from thousands of fireworks, covered the ground everywhere. Layers of it were intermingled with broken glass and coated in early morning dew. The predominant colour was red. It ran through everything like veins. Splashes of it sprung out from the blues and whites. There was even a hint of purple.

The remnants of the night's celebrations would linger for weeks. A broken shard from a champagne bottle could hide in a crevice and perhaps not be found for years. In the distance, down the end of the road, a street-sweeper rounded the corner. Its noisy brushes swished loudly on the pavement. The street cleaners had started working, their thankless task already underway. Somebody always had to clean up the mess. It wouldn't clean itself. Their work would go on for hours, days and weeks before all the mess was gone.

Prince shook his head. The way the living behaved was disappointing. Just to think, he had been one of them once. Had he also been so destructive? He supposed so. Who was he kidding? He could preach from the grave all he liked but nobody would hear.

Then something stopped him in his tracks. A surprisingly clear memory flashed through his head. He closed his eyes and let himself sink into it. Someone was giving him a badge. They pressed it forcefully into the palm of his hand. He was being honoured. What deserving deed had he done? He sensed some doubt. What was being bestowed on him wasn't really an honour. It felt empty. There was a deal going on. Both he and the presenter had mutual needs, the badge a meaningless symbol.

He looked around the room. There were a few large couches and a huge desk. The room itself was unusual. It was perfectly circular. Running along one half of the curved walls was a row of narrow, floor-to-ceiling windows. On the opposing side, a series of doors.

The man was now vigorously shaking his hand. He wore an enormous smile. It was all teeth. Yet the smile didn't convey joy, or any emotion at all for that matter. It was fake. They were both there for the wrong reasons. They were both undeserving of their respective prizes. They had wangled their way into their present positions. He sensed they were very important positions. Could they wangle their way out? No, he realised they couldn't. There was trouble coming. The route which they had chosen to follow, and the manner in which it had brought them there, would lead to their respective downfalls.

The memory faded as suddenly as it had appeared. He opened his eyes and looked down at Anaïs. She was responsible for this. She was bringing the memories back. Being near her had brought this on. He shuffled close to her.

'Don't crowd me,' she snapped.

She was irritated. He was pushing too hard. He took a step away. He would have to tread carefully. His need was too great. If he became too insistent, she could take it all away in an instant.

Old, long-buried memories were coming back. And

only because of her. He had to stick with her. The picture would eventually become clear, whatever it was. He needed her, but what he wanted wouldn't come without a cost. He was indebted to her. As with all things there was no taking without giving. What did she need? He wouldn't get his desires without providing something in return. There was an unspoken pact. They were in this together.

He looked down the road again. At the end of the street the cleaners had moved on and around the corner, but the street wasn't totally devoid of life. Two figures, a man and a dog, stood at the far end. It was no ordinary dog being taken for a walk. Standing by its side was no ordinary man. They had a sense of purpose.

The dog sniffed the air. The man seemed to be searching for something. He studied the ground at his feet. Then he raised his eyes and followed the dotted dividing line which split the road. It led him directly to the ground beneath their feet. Prince held his non-existent breath. The man looked squarely at them. First at the little witch by his side and then up at him.

Prince watched the look on his face transform from deadpan to instant recognition. The man cracked a wry smile. The Inquisitor had found what he was looking for.

CAT AND MOUSE

The dog's nostrils flared. Even from where they were standing, Prince and Anaïs could hear the sound of its heavy breathing. It was like the puffing of an approaching steam train. The Inquisitor adjusted his stance, anchoring his feet in preparation for the chase. The dog mimicked him.

This was going to be difficult. Both sides knew it. You can't hide forever in a city this small. However, you can avoid being caught. Particularly if you have an intimate knowledge of your surroundings. The city's streets were narrow. It was compact. If you were clever, you could twist and turn and stay one step ahead. Speed wasn't necessary; agility was, along with patience and stamina. As long as you could dodge and duck you would not be caught. Then again, you could never completely escape. If you left the relative safety of the canals and alleyways and ventured out into the open suburbs, you became easy prey.

They now stood on the border between the outer and inner city. The wide road encircled the city centre like a belt. To escape, they would have to dive back into the labyrinth of the old city.

Prince glanced down at Anaïs. She was light. That was a blessing. The ability to sustain prolonged physical effort was on his side. He didn't have a heart that would give out on him. He didn't have legs that would tire. He wouldn't get out of breath. In a chase he had a distinct advantage over the Inquisitor. The dog was another thing altogether. If they were to escape the beast, he would have to move fast.

He judged the best way to pick her up. He thought about how to carry her so as to give himself the greatest freedom of movement. He sank down slightly, bending his knees. He coiled his body like a spring. He sought the best possible purchase with the ground. He screwed his boots down through the dirty, wet paper coating the surface of the street. They scraped the solid, rough veneer of the road beneath.

Anaïs looked up at him. 'What are we going to do?'

He lowered his voice to a whisper even though he could not be heard. '*Run,*' he said.

That was enough. She didn't need any further instruction. He opened his arms and she sprang into them.

The dog saw it first. It leapt from a standing start. All four legs left the ground and swiftly come back down as its leash stretched taut. It yelped and turned to the Inquisitor. It howled and gnashed its teeth, drooling saliva. Great globs of it slapped the ground. Entrail-like strands of spittle trailed from its jaws. It strained, dragging its master along behind it.

The Inquisitor's boots slid over the pulped paper until they dug themselves in beneath it. The beast tugged vainly at its invisible leash. The chain around the Inquisitor's hand looped tightly over itself. As the dog strained he felt it crushing his hand. He clenched his fist tighter and fought the pain, forcing his palm wide to prevent the bones from splintering.

He ignored the animal and watched them move.

She had her arms around his neck. The shade pivoted on one leg. The sole of his boot scraped the ground as it twisted in the dirt. He set his other leg down and pushed off. He bounded like a gazelle. His coat billowed out behind him. She let the blanket slip from her shoulders and fall.

The Inquisitor closed his eyes. He pursed his lips and exhaled. He didn't move. Only his straightened arm twitched spasmodically from side to side in front of him. The dog continuing to tug on its leash. He heard their footfalls. Even on the soft, wet surface they echoed down the street, speeding up and gradually fading in the distance.

This would not do.

He needed a better plan. He had to think this

through. He had to get much closer and required the element of surprise to attain his goal. Otherwise, he would squander his energy for naught and be left chasing his own tail.

ON THE RUN

P rince weaved through the streets. He tried to put as much space between them and their foe as he could. He didn't know the consequences of being caught, but they wouldn't be good.

He had never felt real fear as a shade. There was nothing to fear. After all, he was already dead. What harm could come to him? He sensed that possibly the man and his dog had the power to end his existence. Perhaps they weren't just after Anaïs. He wasn't ready to go yet. He still had something to do. If he couldn't get that done, things would not be in balance. He would be incomplete. He had a goal and seeing it to fruition was of primary importance. He would risk everything to achieve it. If only he could work out what *it* was.

But he was only hypothesising. Whatever the man and the dog wanted was a mystery for the moment. It involved her and that was all he needed to know. He had to keep her safe so that she could help him.

He threw a furtive eye over his shoulder. Where were

they? They weren't following. Why? He was certain the dog could have run them down if it was let loose. What were they missing? Was there a trick he hadn't thought of?

He hadn't had time to think it through. It had all been automatic and about self-preservation. It was good they had escaped, but they had to stay that way. They needed to think ahead. They had to devise a plan. They must get as far away as possible, and quickly. There was only one thing for it; they needed some form of transport. He couldn't keep running forever. His legs alone weren't fast enough. The man and his dog had found them once and they would do it again. Only the next time he didn't think they would be as fortunate.

But he was a shade. He couldn't buy a train ticket. He couldn't board a plane. He couldn't hire a car, even if he could have driven one.

He shifted the little witch's weight to his other hip and searched for shelter. Her arms were slung around his neck, which eased the burden. Someone set off a firework down a side street. The loud crack gave him a start. She buried her face in the nape of his neck. The city wasn't completely dead.

He crossed a bridge over a narrow canal, nearly losing his footing on the wet cobblestones. He spotted a public urinal on the edge of the canal. It was a simple structure. A circular, perforated, metal screen around a concrete enclosure built for one. They could hide in there and he could still keep an eye out through the slits in its sides. He slowed his pace and stepped inside. It stank.

'Eeeuw!' Anaïs screwed up her face and pinched her nose.

'*Sorry.*' Prince set her down. He straightened and arched his back. It was more a natural reflex than anything. He had sensed her weight and the exertion of running but felt none the worse for it. It was as if he had expelled no energy at all. The stench of the urinal was also something which failed to arouse any sensory reaction. Looking around the small cubicle he was secretly thankful for one small blessing in being dead.

'Why did you stop?' Anaïs enquired with a muffled voice, her hand still covering her nose and mouth.

'*This is no good. We can't keep running.*' Prince peered apprehensively through the metal latticework. '*We need to get out of the city,*' he said.

Anaïs dropped her hand. 'How do you want to do that?'

'*I was hoping you could solve that problem.*' He looked down at her. '*I was thinking maybe you have something. You are a witch, after all.*'

She growled slowly at him, 'Yes.'

They stood in silence for a moment.

'*Well?*'

Anaïs frowned. 'I don't know. I'd need to think about it. I can't just snap my fingers.'

'*Don't you have a broomstick hidden away somewhere?*'

Anaïs retorted with irritation, 'We don't use broomsticks!'

BROOMSTICKS

The most obvious misconception concerning witches is the broomstick. Where this idea originally sprang from is unknown. The first documenting of it is in a painting by Pieter Bruegel the Elder. A woman is sitting on a broomstick and flying up a chimney. It's a mystery why this particular image was singled out and then popularised. There are all manner of strange creatures flying around on various other objects in the same painting. Perhaps it's because it's an everyday object and the identity of its pilot is concealed.

Witches have been around for millennia; brooms have not. They are a more recent invention. Had they been invented earlier, they may have helped save some civilisations from being inundated by the desert sands. Witches have no need for such things. If your house can be kept spotless by casting a simple spell, what need have you of a cleaning device? The vacuum cleaner was also a bi-product of a spell gone wrong. The inventor would never have made the discovery if it hadn't been for a slight mishap. The original air-powered cleaner blew and didn't suck. It was also so large that it had to be drawn by a horse.

The association of the broomstick with witch transportation is a modern fallacy. The popularity of the idea has more to do with Walt Disney than with anything else. Not to mention a certain indomitable, prepubescent boy. But it is just too obvious. If you saw someone balanced precariously on a stick, screaming across the heavens, you would be shocked, to say the least. Witches do not go out of their way to attract attention to themselves. That would be counter-productive. It is the things you don't see that have the most influence. Subtlety is a more effective weapon.

People are easily threatened by things they don't understand. They will generally refuse to cooperate if presented with something foreign and not within their personal field of knowledge. The living prefer to make fully informed decisions. They don't tend to take strange behaviour or occurrences at face value. Naturals are naturally inquisitive and will go looking for answers. They will start an investigation if something doesn't make sense. An illusion only works if the subject is oblivious to what is really going on. The moment something becomes questionable, belief is no longer suspended. At this point the effectiveness of a spell or potion loses its impact.

No matter how powerful an incantation is, if something is revealed about its actual workings, it will fail. If a subject suddenly gets a glimpse behind the curtain, if they can see what's going on backstage, they will concentrate on uncovering more of its inner workings. They will delve deeper. The desired effect will be lost.

If an illusion goes awry, it is not impossible to rectify it. However, it requires a hell of a lot more work to correct a botched spell, and you just don't want to go there. A whole series of distractions will be required before the original goal can be pursued again. It necessitates an entirely new plan and approach. It's time consuming and difficult. And who wants to do all that extra work?

I've said this before, and I'll say it again: witches are inherently lazy and will go for the easiest possible solution. A set of abnormal circumstances is never helped when the subject notices something out of the ordinary. Unusual objects used for powered flight fall into this category.

Broomsticks attract too much attention. That's not to say other everyday objects haven't been repurposed at one time or another. Witches are not immune to experimentation and have been known to try outlandish solutions on occasions. However, they prefer to keep their secrets to themselves. Sometimes this can go amiss.

Take, for example, the lubricant WD-40. It was originally concocted to ward off the common cold. Unfortunately, curing this disease necessitates a surprisingly complicated spell. In order to treat it an all-encompassing concoction was needed. One of the living got hold of the recipe and now WD-40 has become a cure-all for the strangest things, from pimples to relieving the pain of bee stings. Fortunately, witches have done their best to conceal its original purpose. Now that I have said this, I hope you will honour our agreement and keep this information to yourself. Some potions are just too well made.

Apart from the attention-attracting problem, broomsticks are uncomfortable and difficult to steer. The mere idea of balancing on a stick, even if it's not moving at high speed, seems downright illogical. It's counterproductive. There are much better forms of transportation. For that matter, even a vacuum cleaner is preferable. Although if it is already being drawn by a horse, riding on one is self-defeating and pointless. You might as well just use the horse.

Or, better yet, let someone else provide the transportation.

TRANSPORTATION

Catching a plane would have been the quickest escape route for the pair, but a whole series of obstacles would need to be overcome. For instance, there is the complication of passports and such. If you are dead, you forfeit the right of citizenship. And if you are without country, you are also without a passport. Forgeries can be come by, but they take time. But, if you're a shade, you can't be photographed. Your image will not show up on film. If you're lucky, you'll show up as a white smear, but only if you have a particularly strong aura. Passport control are certainly not going to let you through on the basis of a blank photograph. They ask questions, and, as a shade, you can't answer them.

This is also one reason why airport terminals are so full. There are great numbers of shades hanging around and hoping to get somewhere. Any destination is better than none at all. Once inside, they realise that catching a flight is impossible. However, the comfort of being part of a crowd keeps them there. If airport staff were aware of this it might help them solve the problem of overcrowding in terminals.

Driving a car was also out of the question. There are some things Prince could physically do and others not. He could touch Anaïs, but only because she was a witch. A natural would not be influenced in the same way. At best they can sense a shade. They will feel the cold that is exuded. Inanimate objects can be moved, but this requires enormous concentration. It's a talent which is bestowed on some shades, but there are limitations. Only one object can be moved at a time. A car is a fairly complex contraption and requires you to control multiple integrants at once. It goes far beyond the capabilities of the dead.

Anaïs and Prince stepped out of the urinal and stood on the edge of the canal. The stench had become unbearable and Anaïs couldn't take it anymore. Even witches can't hold their breath forever. She had her straw, but it only filtered air; it didn't mask offensive odours. The musty fetidness wafting up from the murky waters at her feet was little better. Standing on the embankment high above the water, Anaïs felt exposed. They had to find shelter quickly. The man and his dog could be anywhere.

Anaïs consulted her promptuary. She opened it and spoke into it. 'Map.'

The pages flickered and a map of the city materialised on them.

'Zoom out,' said Anaïs.

The promptuary obliged and the city of Amsterdam

shrank. The book displayed a complete map of north-western Europe. The British Isles caught her eye. It pulsed with a faint red glow. Anaïs took it as a sign; it was indicating where they should go.

Great! she thought.

The last time she had been in England, she'd had a problem with the small matter of an Empire State Building in the wrong place. The Rolling Stones concert was another thing she could never live down. Even though those events were mishaps and not entirely successful, they were only illusions. She was reminded that tricks of the eye are powerful but not true magic. To stay one step ahead of their pursuers, she would need more than an illusion. Prince had been correct in his appraisal of their situation. They would need to get as far away as possible.

A movement further down on the opposite side of the canal caught her attention. A man was cleaning a boat. The vessel was a reasonably sized motorised sloop. A horizontal, purple stripe ran the full length of its grey hull. Anaïs's eyes lit up. The remnants of a string of exploded fireworks decorated the bow and empty cans rolled around on the deck. The man was collecting all the rubbish and stuffing it in a plastic garbage bag.

'Let's go,' said Anaïs. She set off and Prince followed. They crossed the bridge they had sprinted across earlier and picked their way along the water's edge, all the while vigilant for other signs of life. They reached the moored sloop and stood on the embankment above it. The man noticed them standing there and looked up.

'Careful you don't fall in.'

Anaïs smiled down at him. 'Thanks, I'll look out.'

He eyed the little girl suspiciously. 'You're up and about early,' he said.

The man, in his early thirties and decked out in a white captain's shirt with stiff lapels, turned his attention to Prince. The shade stared apathetically out across the canal, seemingly oblivious to the presence of the man on the boat.

'Is he ok?' The boatman pointed at Prince. 'Your grandfather looks a bit worse for wear.'

Anaïs raised an eyebrow. 'Grandfather?'

She looked up at Prince. *'He sees what he wants to see, remember. You are a child. He fills in the rest. A small child would only be out with her grandfather on a day like this. Everyone else would be nursing a hangover.'*

Anaïs nodded slowly and then more vigorously at the boatman. 'Yes, my grandfather.' She screwed up her lip. 'He's ok. We didn't get much sleep last night.'

'Doesn't surprise me. I don't think anyone could sleep through the racket.' He cursed under his breath. 'They should ban the whole thing. What is there to celebrate anyway?'

Anaïs shrugged and studied the boat. It looked sturdy enough. She had no nautical knowledge but surmised that it should get them across the channel. She only had to convince the boatman to take them.

Anaïs beamed her most angelic smile. 'Do you mind if we come aboard?'

The boatman looked sceptically up at Anaïs and Prince.

'Please?' she pleaded and flashed her teeth at him.

The boatman's face softened. 'I suppose it will be ok for a moment.'

'Cool,' said Anaïs with enthusiasm. 'I've never been on a boat like this before.'

The boatman moved to the edge of the vessel and close to the embankment. He extended his hand up to her. Anaïs grabbed it and jumped down into his arms. He grunted and nearly lost his footing. He cursed under his breath again.

She had her arms around his neck. He pulled his face away from hers, narrowed his eyes and scowled at her. 'You better warn me if you're going to do that again.' He bent over and deposited her on the deck. He turned to assist Prince and choked with surprise. The shade was standing right next to him. The boatman's eyes widened and he cleared his throat uncomfortably. Prince looked straight through him. The boatman cautiously backed away from the shade without taking his eyes off him.

Anaïs took off her beret and turned her back to them. She rummaged around in the hat. She found what she was looking for: the little silver box from the apothecary. She pulled it out.

Tentatively, the boatman turned his eyes away from Prince and looked down at Anaïs. 'What's that?'

'Lollies, candy. Do you want one?'

He thought for a moment. She gave him her best smile. Reluctantly, he agreed. 'I suppose so.'

'I've got some different ones. What's your favourite?'

'Zoute drop.'

'I prefer the sweet, soft liquorice myself, but I know many people like the sour ones. I think you might be lucky. Let me have a look.'

She opened the box and selected one of the various coloured balls rattling around inside. She held out her hand. There was a single black piece of salmiak liquorice, in the form of a cat, cupped in the centre of her palm. The boatman hesitated.

She sensed his trepidation. 'It's really yummy. Personally I prefer the purple ones, so you can't have one of those.'

He relented, took the sweet and examined it carefully. He eyed Anaïs, decided she was on the level, and popped it in his mouth.

'Mmm, you're right, it's really good.' He bit into the sweet and his eyes glazed over. A vapid grin spread across his face.

She waved her hand in front of his face. There was no reaction. He didn't even blink. He was as catatonic as Prince's camouflage.

'We are going to England,' announced Anaïs.

A serious look replaced the stupid grin. He pulled himself up to his full height and puffed out his chest. He nodded slowly.

'We are going to England,' repeated the boatman.

ON THE HIGH SEAS

The boat was bigger than she had expected. A cabin arose amidships. Inside was a kitchen, and, deeper under the deck, an open door led to a bedroom. The boat was solid and appeared seaworthy. Still, Anaïs knew, even before they had left the confines of the North Sea Channel, they would be in for a rough ride. She watched the city of Amsterdam recede into the distance. It looked grey and lifeless. The festivities of the previous night had left their mark. The city was drained. She had thought she would regret leaving, but as the last church spire disappeared behind the smokestacks of the industrial area in the western suburbs, she felt nothing.

She put it down to the loss of Nan. There was no reason for her to stay in the city. She had no real connection to it; only to one very special occupant. With Nan gone, Amsterdam meant nothing to her. She reassured herself that she had a new companion, but

Prince wasn't the same. He was no Nan and, unfortunately, he was dead.

She pulled the silver tin out of her beret again and counted the number of balls. If her calculations were correct she would have just enough to get them across the Channel. She had others—yellow, green, purple— but they had other purposes.

'What are you doing?'

Anaïs was lost in thought and the voice in her head made her jump. She would never get used to it. It was one thing to listen to your own thoughts but, even though Prince couldn't read them, having his voice in there as well felt like an invasion of privacy.

Prince sat next her on the seat at the stern of the boat and looked over her shoulder.

'Just checking whether I have enough supplies.'

'And do you?'

Anaïs pursed her lips. 'No, not really, but I know a place. This will have to do for now. We have enough to make it to the other side.' She thought for a minute. 'Can you lay your hands out on your lap?'

'Why?' He eyed her with suspicion.

She smiled at him. 'Just humour me. It won't hurt. I want to try something.'

He shrugged and did as requested.

Anaïs pulled her legs up and knelt on the seat. She turned to face him. 'Palms up, please.'

He obeyed. She put the tin next to her on the seat and pulled out her promptuary. She opened it and laid it flat on his hands. Immediately the open page transformed into a screen and, once again, a map appeared on the page. A flashing dot now showed their current position. The map zoomed out to show an overview of Western Europe and the British Isles. It then zoomed in on the south coast of England. A second spot appeared and started to blink. It was somewhere in Cornwall. She looked up at his face. 'Do you know this place?'

He shook his head. *'No.'*

She studied the map closely. 'I think the promptuary is showing us where you need to be.' She looked up at him. 'I think if we can get you there, we can solve what needs to be solved.'

He nodded with uncertainty and twisted the corners of his mouth. *'You may be right.'*

Anaïs tried to reassure him. 'It's definitely trying to tell me something. It has been doing strange things since I met you.' She put her hand on his shoulder. 'I think it knows what we have to do.'

Anaïs felt his shoulder relax. *'I suppose we have nothing else to go on, do we?'* Prince grinned and leant back in the seat. *'Let's just go with it.'*

Anaïs beamed. 'Excellent!'

She took a ball out of the silver tin. She closed its lid before dropping it in her beret and pulling the hat firmly down on her head. She stood up on the seat and stepped across to the boatman. Both his hands firmly gripped the boat's wheel and his gaze was fixed on the canal as it widened ahead of them. He was oblivious to her presence. Anaïs yanked down on his chin and threw the ball in his mouth. She then clamped his jaw shut.

Taking the book from Prince's lap she held it in front of the boatman's face.

'Take us there,' she commanded, pointing at the flashing dot on the map.

He sucked nonchalantly on the ball and stared at the spot she indicated in the book. He shrugged. 'Ok.'

She closed the promptuary, dropped it back in her jacket pocket, and jumped down from the seat. She carefully picked her way along the gunwale and sat at the bow. It was colder out on the water than it had been on land and she pulled her jacket tightly around her. She wished she had not dropped the blanket.

Anaïs shut her eyes and let the wind play in her hair. They were leaving the canal and heading out into open water. The wind strengthened and buffeted her. Occasionally sea spray flew over the bow and splattered her face. She didn't mind. Its bite was invigorating. She opened her eyes, stared at the waves and kept a lookout for other vessels.

Prince wished he could sit next to her but she needed time alone. He visualised the flashing dot in the promptuary and felt a spark of hope ignite inside him. Something told him it wouldn't be long before he had a new future.

THE CROSSING

The English Channel is a dangerous place, especially in a small boat. There are ferries, hydrofoils and transport ships of all sizes and descriptions. Most of them are a great deal larger than a sloop. It's not a place for the faint hearted. As with most wide bodies of water, it also attracts less than ideal weather conditions.

Anaïs had been prepared for a rough ride but had not expected it to be so severe. Once they had hit the open seas, she realised it was not wise to remain at the bow. She had taken shelter in the cabin. She stood on the kitchen table, gripped a railing on the bulkhead and peered out through a small porthole towards the prow of the boat. The swell was whipping the little boat from side to side. It struggled over the break of a wave and down the other side. Water washed up over the head and crashed against the porthole, obscuring her view. Anaïs instinctively pulled back from it. The sea water ran down the porthole and harmlessly over the sides of the boat. She turned toward the stern and peered through the open door at the boatman. His stony face was contorted in deep concentration. She was certain that if he hadn't been under the influence of the potion, his face would have also been clouded with fear.

He struggled at the helm, gunning the engine as the sloop climbed the face of a particularly large wave. He rode the sea's undulations, flexing his knees as the vessel bucked under his feet. Prince sat behind him on the aft seat. He looked out grimly at the sea, his hands firmly clasping the seat cushion on either side of his legs. If he hadn't been dead, his hands would have displayed the whites of his knuckles. He turned to face her and she gave him a reassuring smile. It was half-hearted. He didn't buy her false confidence and she saw the worry in his eyes, even through the camouflage.

She returned to staring out the porthole and riding the table like a surfboard. Keeping one eye on the sea, she pulled out her promptuary. She flipped it open with her free hand and balanced it on her palm.

'Map,' she said.

The book obliged, its pages transmogrifying into a screen once more. It zoomed out from their position. They were approximately midway across the Channel. Threat of the ocean and inclement weather or not, there was no point in turning back now.

She spoke into the promptuary, her voice wavering. She hoped the book could not sense fear. 'Zoom out,' she commanded.

As earlier, she was presented with an overview of the British Isles. The dot in the southwest corner of the country still blipped. They were a long way away from it. Anaïs scrutinised the coastline and decided it was best if they headed directly for it. She was no expert, but common sense told her the seas should be calmer closer to the shore. She traced her finger along the contours of eastern Britain until she found the town closest to their present position, Lowestoft.

She looked out through the porthole and waited for a lull in the sea. When it came she sprang down from the table and made her way to the stern. She climbed onto the seat next to Prince and thrust the promptuary into the boatman's face. He snapped out of his trance-like demeanour, refocusing his eyes on the book. Anaïs pointed at the town.

'Take us here,' she yelled, trying to make herself heard above the roar of the waves churning around them. The boatman nodded and dropped his eyes to a compass embedded in the steering console. He looked from book to compass and back again, adjusting their course. Anaïs dropped the promptuary in her pocket, took the beret off her head and retrieved the silver tin. She pried the boatman's jaws open, which was quite difficult, considering he was gritting his teeth. She popped a black ball in his mouth and watched him roll it around with his tongue.

Satisfied he wasn't going to spit it out, she resealed the tin, dropped it back into the beret and pulled it securely down around her ears. She looked down at Prince.

He studied her face. *'Problem?'* he enquired.

'No.' Her voice thick with sarcasm. She waved her arm at the surrounding water. 'I don't like this. Do you?'

Prince slowly shook his head. *'No.'*

She pulled the promptuary from her pocket, flipped it open and ordered it to display the map. She shoved the book in his face.

'Look.' She pointed to the town of Lowestoft. 'We've set a course to bring us closer to the coast. I think we'll have calmer water there.'

'Seems logical to me and I hope you're right. But once we're there, then what?'

'We'll just skirt the coast until we get to your little dot.' She indicated the flashing speck on the map.

He looked up at her quizzically and shook his head. *'It's not my dot.'*

She nodded enthusiastically and grinned down at him. 'Oh, I think it is.' She put a hand on his shoulder. 'Either way, we're going to make it yours.'

They fell silent and joined the boatman in staring towards the bow. The vessel was broadsided by a wave and Anaïs instinctively grabbed the boatman's arm to stop herself being launched out of the vessel. He lost his footing and had to re-centre his balance, clutching the wheel tightly for support. Prince slid his arm around her legs and a chill run up them. She decided to put up with the cold. Any contact at all was a welcoming comfort right now.

LAND HO

T he boatman held the sloop at a constant distance from land for a long time. Darkness had fallen, but occasionally the full moon peeked out from between the clouds and showed them their surroundings. As they skirted the coast she began to make out wide expanses of beach and the outline of rolling hills in the distance. There didn't seem to be any comforting lights indicating civilisation.

Anaïs had expected to see more evidence of life on the shoreline. In the semi-darkness it all seemed so barren and uninhabited. A little further down the coast was a reassuring indication of life: a lighthouse swept the sea.

She consulted her promptuary. The current had carried them south from her original objective, the town of Lowestoft. They were also still far from their intended destination. It was slow going, and she estimated it would take days to get there using their present mode of transportation.

She looked over the boatman's shoulder and inspected the fuel gauge on the console in front of him. It was plunged deep into the red. They were barely running on fumes and needed to put in to shore. The needle swung with the rocking of the boat. Every now and then it passed above the empty mark before sweeping back down through the red and hitting rock-bottom. It wouldn't be long before they would be helplessly adrift. She could swim, but not far. She wondered if the dead could swim. She supposed it was unnecessary. Prince could probably just walk along the seabed if he wanted to. But even if that were possible it didn't help her. She couldn't take a stroll along the sea floor with him. She thought about the straw, but it wouldn't be of any use. It only purified air, it didn't supply the stuff.

Anyway, abandoning the boat wasn't an option. There was a natural involved and she couldn't risk the life of the boatman. It would go against the most fundamental rule of witchdom, the sheltering of the living from the unknown. He was an innocent pawn. She had borrowed him to achieve a goal and had no right to take his life. This was not something she wanted to consider. It made her squeamish. She didn't want to be responsible for the death of yet another person.

She resigned herself to their predicament. Getting to their destination by sea was impossible. Even if they could find a port and put into it, they would have to refuel. This would mean bringing unwanted attention to themselves. Things were complicated enough as they were. It was far easier if they remained incognito. They would just have to beach the boat somewhere and search for another means of transport. Perhaps they could hitch a ride with someone else.

Anaïs jumped down from the seat and went to the side of the boat. She peered over the edge. The water was dark. It looked cold and uninviting, even if swimming had been a viable course of action.

Prince was looking at her. He had also seen the fuel gauge. *'We can't stay out here very much longer.'*

She acknowledged him with a nod. 'Yes I know. I was just considering our options.'

'I know.'

Her eyes widened. 'Oh? Can you read my mind now?'

He smirked. *'No, it's obvious. We have to get to shore.'*

The situation soon resolved itself. Anaïs had forgotten to feed the boatman. He had stood at the helm for hours, engrossed in piloting the vessel. She had been concentrating on the coastline and her promptuary. She had neglected to keep an eye on him and, more importantly, his medication. When it happened, both Anaïs and Prince were unaware of him snapping out of his trance. It took them by complete surprise until he cried out in alarm.

'Hey! What's going on? Where are we?'

The boatman looked around frantically. Prince was standing next to him. The boatman swung around and went to shake the shade. 'Hey! Grandpa!'

The boatman, aiming for Prince's shoulders, went to grab what he thought was a senile old man staring listlessly into space. The illusion was so complete, and he lunged with such force, that he only succeeded in hugging himself and falling headlong through the shade. He knocked his head on the sharp, leading edge of the seat. His shoulder connected with it as well and he bounced off, flipped over and ended up flat on his back on the deck. A trickle of blood ran down the side of his face. Sheer panic set in.

'What ...' His lips quivered. 'Who are you? Where am I?'

He scrabbled frantically for purchase. Still on his back, he kicked his legs and shimmied around on the deck like a crab, attempting to put some distance between himself and the shade. He only succeeded in jarring his head once more against the bulkhead, this time at the little witch's feet.

'Help!' he cried.

Anaïs stood over him and tried to calm him. She put her finger to her lips.

'Shh, it's ok,' she said.

She used the most soothing voice she possessed but it came out all wrong. It only confused him even more. Five-year-olds don't talk like husky harlots.

He threw her a bewildered look and shrank away from her. He scrambled into a corner and as far away from them as physically possible. In the cramped confines of the boat there was no real escape. He pulled himself up and peered over the side towards the coast. They were passing the mouth of a wide bay flanked by low headlands on either side.

'This isn't the Netherlands! Where the hell are we?' cried the boatman.

Anaïs had to act fast. The boatman certainly wasn't going to accept a piece of confectionery from her this time. Now they were on their own. She did the only thing she could do. She sprang up on the seat and grabbed the wheel. She spun it hard toward land. It threw Prince off balance and sent him careening across the boat towards the boatman. The sailor threw up his hands to protect himself and Prince fell through them and into his body. Anaïs saw his frame stiffen with the sudden cold spike which rushed through him as the shade made contact. It was too much for the boatman. He passed out.

Anaïs hung vainly onto the wheel, trying to steady the boat. Fortunately, she guided it between the headlands and into the bay. She peered between the spokes of the steering wheel and waited for her pounding heart to settle. Prince picked himself up and slid across the seat next to her.

He nudged her. '*That was entertaining.*'

She scowled at him.

'Not funny,' she said.

The bay was practically empty. There was a wide crescent beach with a small village nestled at the far end of it. Its lights winked at her. There was no harbour, just sand and pebbles. The engine cut out when they were a few metres from the shore and they had to wait until the tide carried them up onto the beach. An especially large swell lifted them up and unceremoniously dumped them high above the waterline. Thankfully, Anaïs was prepared for the impact and had wrapped her entire body around the wheel. She heard the crunch of the sand and stones as the bottom of the boat crashed down on the beach. The sea receded and left them high and dry.

They had no choice but to leave the boatman lying in his vessel. He was too heavy for her to move. Anaïs felt a bit awkward leaving him there. The best she could do was give him an idea where he was. She rummaged in her beret, found a pen and piece of paper, and scrawled a word on it: England. She stuffed it in the half-clasped palm of his hand.

Anaïs dropped down from the boat. Her shoes buried themselves in soft sand. She shook her legs one at a time to extract them. Prince landed silently beside her and gave her a start. They both trudged around the stern of the boat and looked down the beach. The welcoming lights from the village beckoned from the other end of the bay. The full moon shook itself free of clouds and bathed the beach in monochrome light. She narrowed her eyes.

Halfway between them and the village were two figures on the hard sand close to the waterline. Waves crashed on the beach around them, creating a fine mist. She watched them materialise slowly out of the spray. It was a man and a dog.

The dog was enormous, almost half the height of the man. Even though it wasn't particularly cold, and in spite of the mist, heat haze rose from it. The beast growled, the sound echoing around the bay. Anaïs froze to the spot in horror. Then the animal began running towards them.

This time the Inquisitor didn't hold it back. The chain hung slack in his hand. A joyless grin split his face.

A SAVIOUR IN STILETTOS

Prince and Anaïs thrashed their way up through the brush bordering the beach. It wasn't particularly high or thick but it inhibited her movement. She didn't have the size or strength to get through it effectively. She fought on, though. She had to.

All the while she thought about the figures on the beach. How had they found her? How had they got to England before her? And, most of all, who were they? She still had no answers.

One foot sank through spongy grass and into water. It was bitterly cold and seeped through her shoe. She let out a cry of surprise and then muffled it with her hand. They mustn't hear her. She stopped and listened. The brush around them was silent. This was good. It meant they weren't close.

She was convinced the dog would make a lot of noise. It was at least as tall as her and much heavier. She would certainly hear it as it forced its way through the thick undergrowth. Out in the open they would have been caught immediately. In the dense shrubbery they were on an even footing. It was the only way off the beach, and if they were somewhere in there with her and Prince, then their progress would also be inhibited.

Anaïs tried to ignore her wet foot and struggled onwards. Within minutes they burst through an especially thick section of brush and out into the open. She and Prince had stumbled onto a narrow country laneway. It was like being released from a prison and the stiffness in her shoulders relaxed. The stress ebbed. She caught her breath and looked up and down the lane. She was reasonably sure of her bearings from the flash of the lighthouse in the night sky and elected to turn left. It would take her away from the village and their pursuers. Now they were in the open they could move faster, but their advantage wouldn't last long. They had to keep moving. Once the Inquisitor and his dog found their way out of the brush, they would be upon them in no time.

The blaring honk of a car horn made her jump. A black Morris Minor skidded to halt on the damp road, gliding sideways in the mud which coated it. It only just stopped short of hitting them. Its engine coughed and died. The vehicle's windows were fogged with condensation and Anaïs couldn't make out its occupants. The driver cranked down the window, the winder squeaking loudly. A woman stuck her head out. It was the librarian.

Anaïs and Prince looked at one another. He raised an eyebrow.

The librarian scowled at Prince. 'Is he still hanging around with you?'

Anaïs shrugged and pulled a face at the woman in the car.

The librarian pursed her lips and knotted her eyebrows. She sighed. 'I expect you need some assistance?'

Anaïs and Prince held their ground. Both were surprised to see the woman and unsure if her question was meant as an invitation. Was she offering to help? Her coarse disposition sent conflicting signals.

Exasperated by the lack of movement, the librarian yelled with irritation, 'Well, what are you waiting for? Get in!'

Anaïs grabbed Prince and they rushed around to the far side of the vehicle. She struggled with the door lever. It was rusted and wouldn't budge. Prince, unable to offer any physical help, shuffled helplessly on the spot next to her, dancing from one foot to the other.

'Oh, come on!' the librarian cried in earnest. 'Put your back into it.'

Anaïs put one foot on the chassis for leverage. She tugged with all her might. Mercifully, the handle yielded and the door flew open. Anaïs stumbled backwards and was caught by a hedge on the side of the road. She extracted herself and went to shove Prince into the front seat.

The librarian stopped them by raising the palm of her hand. Fluorescent nail polish on the tips of her fingers glinted in the dashboard light. 'No, he goes in the back,' she said forcefully and flipped her thumb towards the rear of the car. 'I'm not having him sit next to me.'

Anaïs gave her a disdainful look but did as requested. She opened the well-greased back door for Prince, closed it behind him and jumped in the front seat. As she slammed her door shut a movement through her window caught her attention. It was the Inquisitor and his dog.

They crashed through the brush a few metres down the road. The Morris Minor's headlights caught them like rabbits in a spotlight. The dog dug in its claws and froze. The Inquisitor, who was unable to stop as quickly as the animal, tripped over it and ended up spread-eagled on the road. He scrabbled quickly to his feet.

Anaïs screamed at the librarian, 'Drive! Now!'

The librarian twisted the key in the ignition. Mercifully the motor roared to life. She gunned the engine, grated the gears and planted a stiletto on the accelerator. The car careened in reverse and into the hedgerow lining the side of the lane. The rear of the vehicle crunched in the bushes. The librarian grabbed the gear lever with both hands, wrenched it out of reverse and jammed it forcefully into first gear, puffing out her cheeks with the exertion. She drove her foot down hard on the accelerator, almost standing in her seat whilst doing so. The car's wheels spun before finding purchase. It extracted itself from the undergrowth, the branches scraping the bodywork like fingernails on a blackboard. The occupants of the Morris Minor all cringed in unison. The vehicle launched itself back onto the road proper, fishtailed on the slippery surface and belted off down the laneway, leaving the Inquisitor and his dog standing flatfooted in the middle of the road.

Anaïs didn't look back, focussing instead on the narrow road ahead, her heart pounding.

NOT ALONE

The librarian was a surprisingly competent driver. She guided the vehicle fearlessly through the narrow country lanes at breakneck speed. A rally driver in stilettos and a miniskirt, she even wore fingerless, black leather driving gloves. Anaïs guessed she never went anywhere without first checking her appearance.

Her attire didn't quite fit the car she was driving. A Ferrari would have suited her more than a Morris Minor. This did not prevent her from driving the little car in the manner of its more expensive Italian cousin. She shifted rapidly up and down through the gears and barely braked. She leant her body as they swung around corners, and transferred her weight with the movement of the car. On particularly wide curves she let the back end of the car drift and then pulled it back at the last minute.

Anaïs could hear Prince being tossed around in the back seat and had serious problems trying to remain in her own. She gripped the edge of her seat with one hand and the door handle with the other. It required all her five-year-old strength to prevent her from being thrown around the vehicle like a rag doll.

The librarian was unperturbed. Her dress sense did little to disguise her cold nature. She ignored her passengers and focussed on the road ahead. The little car hit a hump in the road and became airborne for a moment. It crashed back down on the asphalt, jarring its passengers as the vehicle bottomed out. Its old springs laboured under the strain. The impact took the wind out of Anaïs.

The librarian cleared her throat but didn't offer an apology. She did, however, reduce her speed.

Anaïs caught her breath and spoke first. 'What are you doing here?'

The librarian screwed up her face and spat at her, 'I wish I knew.'

She flashed her eyes at Anaïs before turning back to concentrate on the road ahead. They approached an enormous oak tree. Its bulbous trunk jutted out into the lane. The librarian wrenched on the steering wheel and guided them around it with millimetres to spare. Anaïs bit her lip as it flashed past her window.

The librarian grimaced and then the look on her face softened slightly.

'Well I do actually.' She measured her words. 'Know, that is.'

She looked across at Anaïs again. 'They sent me. The Organisation. They didn't want you left alone.' She sighed. 'It wasn't my choice. I was very happy where I was. But, as they say, it's all for the cause.'

'I suppose I should thank you?' said Anaïs.

The librarian huffed. 'I wouldn't go supposing anything if I were you.'

Anaïs went to shoot back an equally snide remark but thought better of it. The less she said to the woman, the better.

She turned to watch the road. The hedgerows flashed by. They were incredibly close. The narrow country lane was pitch black, the moon having concealed itself behind the clouds, and the Morris Minor's feeble headlights only just cut through the darkness. What little there was of the road tapered. It left only enough room for something slightly bigger than a Morris Minor to pass through. With the overhanging trees providing a canopy, Anaïs had the impression they were in a runaway train barrelling down a tunnel.

Anaïs released her grip on the seat and door handle and searched for some way to anchor herself to the car. She fumbled for her seatbelt and clicked it in place, testing the connection to make sure it was secure. Only then did she settle back into her seat. She closed her eyes and regulated her breathing until her heart's rapid palpitations subsided. She looked up at the librarian who wore a wry smile and seemed to be relishing the moment. She clearly wanted to make Anaïs suffer for her own inconvenience.

Anaïs put on a brave face and straighten in her seat. 'Where are we going?'

The librarian sniffed the air. 'I thought you had a plan?'

Anaïs frowned. 'Um, no, not really.'

'Well you better think of something. I'm just trying to put some distance between us and your friend with the dog.'

Anaïs screwed up her nose. 'He's not my friend.'

The librarian smiled. 'I didn't think so.'

'Are you a witch?'

The librarian feigned embarrassment. 'That's a bit forward of you.' She warmed slightly. 'No, not a real one. We wouldn't be sitting here together if I was. Too much power all in one place and that sort of thing.'

'Yes, you're right. I wasn't thinking.'

The librarian took her foot off the accelerator for a moment and dropped her eyes from the road. She looked squarely at Anaïs. 'I'm just part of the family, kind of in the same way your caretaker was.'

A wave of sadness swept over Anaïs. She didn't want to be reminded about Nan. She expected the librarian to go further and give a jibe about her role in Nan's death. Anaïs was relieved when nothing came. She sensed the librarian's mood was mellowing. She watched the woman ensconce herself deeper in her seat and become less aggressive, completely absorbed with her driving. Perhaps she was also considering the possible deadly ramifications of assisting a witch.

Her calm demure was only temporary. Anaïs watched the librarian become tense again, grit her teeth and slam the car through the next corner. Anaïs sucked air through her teeth and choked on her heart. The

P J WHITTLESEA

librarian's erratic behaviour wasn't instilling Anaïs with much faith.

'Please, take it easy,' she pleaded.

'Ok, I'm sorry.' The librarian slowed the vehicle and let it roll to a stop. She slung one arm over the steering wheel and turned to Anaïs. 'If we're going to spend time together then perhaps you ought to know my name.'

Anaïs could see she was making an attempt to curb her usual sharp nature. 'Yes, that would help. What is it?'

It came as no surprise that her name was as brazen as the rest of her. She puffed herself up. 'Immaculate Phlox,' said the librarian.

Anaïs had to stifle a smile. 'Nice to meet you, Immaculate.'

The librarian stiffened at the sound of her name. 'Please, don't call me that. You sound like my mother. Call me Immi. I'd prefer that. It's a lot less formal.'

She slotted the car into first gear and planted her foot on the accelerator. They roared off into the night with Prince and Anaïs pinned once more to the backs of their seats.

A PLACE FOR THE NIGHT

The bed and breakfast was in an old farmhouse. The entire building creaked and squeaked, not only the floorboards. The house had a life of its own. It wasn't just the walls that chattered; everything had something to say. Anaïs had only caught glimpses of bits of the house as they were escorted to their rooms. The expansive dining room, its walls lined with crockery; the long corridor lined with a threadbare runner; the wonky yet solid staircase that wound its way up through the guts of the building.

The bed Anaïs had been given was ancient; a huge, four-posted double bed. It didn't have a canopy but, nevertheless, had some fairy-tale appeal. She felt like a princess. The quilt and blankets were piled high and swallowed her up. She felt safe with the weight of them pressing down on her. And it was warm. The time at sea had cooled her body and she was still feeling the effects. She rubbed her skin to massage more warmth into it.

As she lay in bed, the house settled and was quiet.

The silence was deafening. The pressure on her eardrums reminded her of the time she had flown with Nan. It had been on their ill-fated trip to London. She recalled the pain in her ears on take-off. She had not wanted the airliner to land for fear of a repeat of the torture. Thankfully the landing proved less unpleasant.

Thoughts of Nan continued to dominate her mind. She had come to accept her death, or at least the idea that there was nothing she could do about it. It was what lay beyond that bothered her now. She wondered where Nan was. Had her caretaker been granted safe passage to another realm or was she like other shades and hanging around on a street corner somewhere? Was she waiting, just like Prince, for her witch to come along so that she could make peace with the world? Anaïs hoped that wasn't necessary. She hoped that Nan didn't have to make peace with anything. But she doubted that. Nan had mother issues which hadn't been resolved. Anaïs didn't think an exception would be made because her mother was a witch. When this was over she would try to find out more. It was her responsibility. Not only that. She was growing in confidence. The afterlife was fast becoming her speciality.

She tried to sleep but her mind continued to whir incessantly. It gave her no rest. She squirmed in the bed. Her feet were cold and she curled up in a ball, pulling her knees up to her chin. She massaged heat into her toes. Then she heard it. At first it was a faint scratching. Irregular and innocent. Then it became more insistent. Loud and regular.

She peeked out from under the covers and in the

half-light she could see Prince sitting by the window. He was seated in a small, wooden rocking chair. It seemed to have been designed for a child and could barely contain him. The bedroom was under the eaves of the house and the only window went from the floor halfway up the wall. It stopped where the slope of the ceiling began. The small chair was in front of it. It appeared built for its position and perhaps not constructed specifically for a child, but scaled down in size so that any occupant could see out the window.

The scratching was coming from the window. It grew louder. The pane of glass hidden behind a roller blind sounded like it was being scored with a house nail. Prince heard it too. It was impossible to ignore. He looked at Anaïs. Their eyes met and she could see the concern in them.

The roller blind whipped up, flapping against the window frame and making them both jump. Outside, sitting on the roof next to the window and peering through it, was a small boy. He held on to the overhanging branch of a nearby tree and was using it to scratch at the glass.

A rather loud voice rang in her head and it wasn't Prince's. *'Are you Anaïs Blue?'*

She could barely bring herself to speak but managed a whisper. 'Yes.'

The boy's eyes shone in the dark. *'I don't want to impose, and realise you're busy, but could you deliver a message for me?'*

Anaïs attempted to subdue her beating heart. Outside the house, in the neighbouring paddock, she had seen a cemetery. It was ancient, with a small collection of tombstones jutting out of the ground at rank angles. The souls there would not have had the advantages of the city. They were quite isolated and wouldn't get many witches in these parts. Anaïs already sensed that if she were to go outside, she would be very popular. After her experience in the streets of Amsterdam she ascertained that hanging out with a shade might be a magnet for others, and somehow they would know she was there. But she hadn't expected one to come looking for her.

It irritated her. What was driving these shades to be so forward all of a sudden? It was rude. Didn't they realise she was battling sleep deprivation? And it would have been more appropriate to first apologise for scaring the hell out of her before making demands.

The boy tapped the glass, *'Miss Blue?'*

This infuriated her even more. 'Please stop calling me that. My name is Anaïs Thistle!'

The boy shrank back from the window. *'Sorry.'*

Anaïs tried to calm herself. She toyed with the idea of telling him to get lost but that would be counterproductive. His insistence clearly communicated that he wouldn't leave without a satisfactory answer.

She pulled the covers around her head like a shawl and sighed. 'I can try to help you.'

The boy smiled. *'Thank you. Sorry for being such a bother. Could you tell my parents I'm fine? Tell them not to worry. It wasn't their fault. Tell them to open their hearts to my sister. Then I will be released.'*

She looked across at Prince. 'Sheesh, he doesn't want much does he?'

Prince was non-committal and shrugged. He didn't want to jeopardise his own chances and thought it better to stay out of the discussion.

Getting no assistance from Prince, Anaïs turned her attention back to the boy. 'Have you been like this for very long?'

The shade moved closer to window and knelt on the apron. *'No, a few months, maybe a year. I'm starting to lose track of time. If you don't help me I may never know what the message is I have to deliver.'*

'He's right,' said Prince. *'That's why I have such a problem.'*

Anaïs snapped at him, 'Oh, *now* you have an opinion!'

Prince regretted speaking up and decided to go with his first strategy. He bit his top lip. Anaïs rolled her eyes at him.

'I think I understand,' said Anaïs to the boy. 'Who and where are your parents?'

'They're downstairs. My mother won't understand, but my father will. He has seen things.'

Anaïs was curious. 'What things?'

'Oh, just things he can't explain. I have tried to communicate with him but it didn't work.'

'What happened to you?'

'I was stupid. I let it all get to me. School, a job, girls … stuff.' He paused, playing it all back through his head. *'I wrapped a car around a truck. The driver should also know it wasn't his fault. My father can tell him.'*

Anaïs was confused. How could such a small boy drive a car?

'How old were you?' she enquired.

'Eighteen.' The shade furrowed his brow. *'Why, don't I look eighteen?'*

'No, I'm afraid you look about ten years younger.' Anaïs sat up in bed and wrapped the covers around her shoulders. 'I'm seventeen,' she said. 'I don't think it's stupid at all. I mean the way you felt. Ending it all might have been a bit extreme, though.' She looked down at the lump of her legs under the covers. Her toes were still cold and she wiggled them in an effort to coax more blood into them. She looked back across at the boy at the window. 'It's hard being this age. You're not the only one. I'm confused and I don't know what to do with my future. And I'm stuck with this.' She pulled her hands out from under the covers and waved them down the length of her body. She let out a deep sigh. 'I want to be with boys but they don't want to be with me.'

'I'm here,' said the boy.

'Me too,' said Prince.

Anaïs gave them a half-smile. 'Thanks, guys, but you're both dead. It's not quite the same.'

The room fell silent, each of them considering their individual predicaments. The shade at the window was the first to break the sombre mood.

'Will you help me?' he enquired cautiously.

Anaïs cleared her throat and composed herself. 'You shades are certainly pushy. Not a lot of sympathy for my situation, I must say.'

'Sorry,' said the boy.

'Stop saying that. We are way beyond apologies. Are you alone out there?'

'As far as I know, yes. I think so.'

'Good, 'cause I need to get some sleep and don't want any more of you tapping at my window. We'll deal with this in the morning. Do you think that would be possible?'

The boy brightened. *'Yes, yes of course.'*

'It's ok, Anaïs, I'll make sure you're not bothered,' said Prince.

Anaïs glared at him. 'You haven't been doing such a good job of it up to now.'

'Don't worry, I will. Now, you get some sleep.'

'Good!' Anaïs pulled the blankets up over her head. 'And goodnight!'

The two shades chimed cheerfully in unison. *'Goodnight!'*

MESSAGES

Not all messages are easy to deliver. At the very least the intended recipient needs to be open to receive it. Some people just refuse to listen. In a world full of chatter some quite important messages get lost. Everybody has something they think is worth saying. However, not everything said is worth being heard.

With this constant cacophony of information we find ourselves shutting things out. Our minds make the most noise. They keep us awake at night with incessant thoughts. Writing it down helps and is another way to get words out into the world. But even then, they get lost. Who still has the time to read?

Years ago it was much simpler. People thought more about what they had to say before they threw the words out there. In the early days of the telephone you couldn't just pick up the receiver and make a call. You had to go via a telephonist. Somebody else had to help you make the connection. If nobody was picking up at the other end, you couldn't leave a voicemail. There were no answering machines. And if somebody didn't want to be contacted they could remain unreachable. They could refuse to answer the phone. Or they could let the mail pile up on their doorstep. There was more control over what was received.

For witches this was an ideal situation. They didn't have to wade through mountains of communication. Like the telephonists of old, they could insert the cable in one line and connect it with another. Of course, there were also fewer people to deal with. There weren't as many cables lying around on the floor and far fewer holes to slot them in to. The population of the planet has grown exponentially and this makes it difficult for wires of any description not to get crossed. Fate has become more important. And witches can't control fate. Like everyone else they can only do the best with what they have at their disposal. They have the tools to narrow down the odds, but even then they still need a willing recipient.

Most people can't handle being confronted with death. Especially if it's standing right in front of them. There are people who are open to that sort of thing. However, they have a tendency to be a little too pushy in their search for the unknown. Desires are not always fulfilled. Especially those which are being forced. Putting pressure on trying to conjure up a spirit can scare it away. Shades are also picky about who they communicate with. After all, they were alive once themselves.

The only real way to make a connection is by

finding something genuine to say. That is why the sender and the receiver need to have a special connection. Only truly heartfelt pleas will be heard. The message has to have a fundamental purpose. Otherwise it's just white noise. Or perhaps pink noise in the case of someone like Anaïs. The communiqué must have substance. The listener needs to be enriched by what they hear. Even shades have difficulty with this. Sometimes what they think they have to say is not really what is required.

Whoever you are, it needs to come from deep within. It must be of some benefit to the listener. This is something a witch can't do for you. They can only establish communication. They don't guarantee success and can't be expected to be your speechwriter. It's up to you to find the right thing to say. And you had better be ready with some pretty wonderful words. The opportunities to truly say the right thing are few and far between.

A WINTER'S MORNING

The early morning snowfall had been heavy. Prince watched from the back seat of the Morris Minor as Anaïs ploughed through it to get to the barn. The farmer had fired up the tractor and it was spewing a plume of black smoke. The smell of diesel hung heavily in the air. He stopped gunning the engine when he saw her approaching.

He climbed down from the cabin and landed with both feet in deep snow. He extracted himself and went to help her over a ditch. He seemed surprised to see her. Prince saw him speak, enquiring if he could help. She beckoned him to come down to her level. He knelt beside her. She pulled him in close by the lapel of his overcoat. Prince watched her yell in his ear to make herself heard over the noise of the tractor. Its low chug thumped the ground and reverberated off the surrounding hills. The farmer straightened, leant back slightly and cracked his spine. He climbed up on the tractor, reached into cabin and cut the engine. Its noise was immediately swallowed up by the deep drifts of snow.

The farmer clambered down from the vehicle and trudged back through the snow. He knelt down beside Anaïs and pulled her in close, wrapping an arm around her shoulders. She shivered from the cold. For a big man, the farmer's movements were very delicate. His body language exuded kindness. He gently picked the little witch up. Holding her tightly in his arms he carried her across to the tractor. He set her down and they huddled together next to it, basking in the ambient warmth of the motor. Anaïs spoke softly to him. The farmer cocked his head, listened intently and studied the expressions on her face.

Prince trained his ears on the conversation but could only catch snippets.

'Son … ok … sorry … forgive,' she said.

She stopped talking, stepped back from the farmer and, with a wave of her hand, indicated something out in the paddock. Prince followed the line of her arm. The landscape was painted entirely white. Fresh snow covered every mound, bush and tree. It was a blank canvas. In the adjoining paddock, amongst a collection of snow-capped tombstones, a solitary black shadow interrupted the white expanse.

The boy stood alone in the centre of the cemetery. Except he wasn't a boy anymore. Miraculously he had taken on his eighteen-year-old form. He was clearly dressed in his funeral attire, an ill-fitting, double-breasted suit. It struck Prince that perhaps the boy was wearing his father's wedding suit. On his head was a tattered baseball cap.

The farmer spotted him. Aghast, he slowly got to his feet. He stood with both arms hanging limply by his side. The initial shock melted from his face. A serenity came over him. Anaïs hovered next to the farmer. She reached across and clasped one of his hands with both of hers. He was oblivious to her presence, his eyes fixed intently on his son. Then their eyes met. Out in the field the boy smiled at his father. The farmer reciprocated. A beatific smile split his face.

The connection was enough. An enormous stag emerged from the treeline at the far end of the paddock and bounded across the snow. It headed straight for the middle of the cemetery. It sprung high over the tombstones and flew at the boy. He held his ground, spreading his arms and clenching his fists. The stag hit the ground behind the boy and the two collided. In an instant the boy became transparent and then disappeared altogether. A wisp of heat haze in the form of the boy hung where he once had been. It too then dissipated.

The stag continued on as if nothing had happened, launching itself over the tombstones and out of the cemetery. It landed on all fours in knee-deep snow and stopped. It turned its great head to face the farm and shook its antlers at the onlookers. It then spun around and darted away, bounding effortlessly through the snow before vanishing into another group of trees.

Tears streamed down the farmer's face. He sniffed and wiped them away with the sleeve of his coat. Prince watched as he mouthed the words 'thank you' at Anaïs. She gave him a sympathetic and reassuring smile, squeezed his hand and nodded.

She left him standing there, staring out into the field, and fought her way through the snow and over to the car. The librarian stood by the driver's door. She was decked out in a mink coat and fur-lined boots. Anaïs looked her up and down.

'My god,' she said. 'Where are these clothes coming from?'

The librarian shrugged.

Anaïs shook her head in bemusement. 'What's up with you, anyway? Do you think we're going to the opera?'

Immi scowled at her.

Great! thought Prince. *This is going to be a fun ride.*

RUN

'So what does it say?'

Anaïs looked first at Immaculate Phlox and then back down at her promptuary.

The librarian continued to push for an answer. 'Well?'

Anaïs was irritated by her tone. She hissed through her teeth. 'It's a bit hard to tell. For some reason I now have two signals. One of them seems to be moving.'

The librarian let out a puff of exasperation. 'Fine, it's moving. That should be a good thing. It means that whatever we are looking for is alive.'

'You may be right, but what troubles me is that it is moving towards us,' said Anaïs.

The librarian smiled, folded her arms and looked straight through the windscreen. 'Excellent, then we don't have to go anywhere. I'm fine with that, especially in this weather.' It had started to snow and a few flakes drifted across the glass and collected on the windscreen wipers. 'It will save us a lot of trouble. Let's just wait for whatever it is to come to us.'

'Can I have a word?'

Anaïs turned to face Prince who sat in the middle of the back seat. He grabbed the two front seats and pulled himself forward.

Immaculate Phlox shuffled in her seat. She tried to move away from the shade but was restricted by her oversized mink coat. 'Don't get so close to me!'

Anaïs ignored the librarian and turned to face him. 'Yes, what is it?'

'We're not alone.'

He pointed through one of the side windows and Anaïs followed the line of his finger. The snow made it easier to track the curve of the road. It made a wide sweep and climbed a nearby hill. On the crown of the hill another car had stopped. It was a large, modern four-wheel-drive. Its front doors were open and spread like wings at its side. The vehicle looked like a huge black bird perched on the crest of the hill. Its occupants had climbed out and were surveying the valley beneath them. Unfortunately, it was now the all-too-familiar sight of a man dressed completely in black and a rather large dog.

Anaïs swore. The librarian went to scold her and decided against it. She saw the fear in the child's eyes. She craned her neck to see out the side window and followed the witch's gaze. In stunned silence all three of them watched the movement on the hilltop.

The Inquisitor pulled what appeared to be a fob

watch out of the folds of his coat. He flipped its cover open and studied it. It was no watch; it was a form of compass. On its face a gold needle swung left and right and then settled. There were several symbols on its circumference. None of them indicated direction.

The Inquisitor turned his body until the point of the needle lined up with one particular emblem. It was the hieroglyph of the goddess Isis. He lifted his head and traced a line from the point of the needle. His eyes followed the road down the hill and settled on a Morris Minor parked near an old farmhouse.

The three occupants of the car stared out the side window and straight into the Inquisitor's scrutinising eyes. He scanned the little car. Anaïs's face was pressed up to her window. There was a moment when her eyes locked with his and she watched in stupefaction as his expression changed. One of his eyebrows rose. He snapped the compass case shut, shoved it in his pocket and barked at the dog. They both leapt into the vehicle.

Anaïs spun in her seat and screamed at the librarian, 'Go!'

She turned and growled at Anaïs, 'Please don't yell at me. And don't *go* me.' She tried to stick a finger in her ear but was prevent from doing so by her manicured fingernail. 'I'll go when I'm good and ready.'

She flexed her fingers and calmly turned the ignition on the little car. There was an unsettling moment of silence, the engine rasped and whined and then burst reassuringly into life. The librarian grinned. She gripped the steering wheel with determination, straightened herself in her seat, and slotted the gear lever into first. The wheels spun momentarily, burying themselves in the snow before finding traction on the tarmac beneath. Fortunately, the librarian had the benefit of foresight and had relieved the farmer of a set of snow chains.

On the crest of the hill the four-wheel-drive had better traction but was hampered by its size. The Inquisitor had to skilfully negotiated its bulk between the snow-laden hedgerows. It required all his concentration. The vehicle's side mirrors clipped every twig and branch but somehow remained intact. He built up speed and let the vehicle glide smoothly around the long curve down the hill. He made it successfully down into the valley.

Once there, the road changed direction, suddenly surprising him. He fought with the steering wheel on the slippery surface. The back end of the vehicle swung out. He swiftly flicked it back. Speeding along the floor of the valley, he no longer had a clear view of the road ahead. Great white globs of snow-covered trees and bushes obscured his view on either side. The narrow road opened out at the entrance to the farm but didn't give him enough time to avoid the object in his path, nor sufficient time to slow the four-wheel-drive.

At the last minute he saw the obstacle and planted both feet on the brake pedal. The back end of the vehicle flew out once again and it slewed sideways. Lifting his hands from the wheel he covered his face with both arms and braced himself for the impact. The four-wheel-drive ploughed into the large rear wheel of the farmer's tractor.

The occupants of the Morris Minor were unaware of their good fortune. By the time the Inquisitor had extracted himself and his dented vehicle from the tractor, and decided he could continue, they were miles away.

CAR TROUBLE

The Morris Minor spluttered and coughed. The librarian pumped the accelerator but it was pointless and only served to make the car lurch down the road. Eventually it ground to a shuddering halt and threw them all forward in their seats.

The librarian slammed her fists down on the steering wheel. 'Damn!'

Anaïs glared at her. 'What happened?'

Immaculate Phlox took a deep breath and tapped the glass cover of the speedometer with a polished fingernail. 'No fuel.'

'No fuel? Why didn't you keep an eye on it?'

With irritation the librarian replied through clenched teeth. 'I was otherwise occupied. There was a little thing about a man and a dog chasing us.'

Anaïs softened. 'Sorry.'

'Can you still see them?'

Anaïs pulled out her promptuary and opened it. 'Map,' she said. The book obliged.

Anaïs studied the map carefully. 'Strange, I only see one dot, the original one. The other one has disappeared.'

'Maybe they're gone,' said Immi.

'Don't bet on it,' said Prince, leaning forward in his seat and giving the librarian a start.

She snapped at him. 'Oh, you're still here?'

Prince chose to ignore her. *'Maybe we can only see them when they're nearby?'*

Anaïs swung around in her seat to face him. 'I hope you're right. Although it's a bit of a worry that we can't track their movements.'

'Hopefully, if we can't see them, then they can't see us.'

Anaïs closed the promptuary. 'Yes, hopefully, but I don't think we can rely on that. We've got to keep moving.'

'Exactly. I don't know what he said but I agree with you,' said the librarian. 'Maybe one day you can let me in on your conversation.' She opened her door. 'I'm going for fuel. We passed a service station not far back. That is, unless you have some trick you can perform?'

Anaïs shook her head. 'I'm afraid not. The internal combustion engine is not my speciality.'

The librarian grabbed the roof of the car. Grunting, she used it to leverage herself up and out of the vehicle. Once she had extracted herself she stood next to the car puffing from the exertion. She leant down and stuck her head back in the vehicle. 'Pity. I would have hoped a witch would be good for something.'

Anaïs shrugged.

The librarian sighed. 'Fine, I'll be right back then. Anyone care for a walk?'

There was no response from the car's occupants. The librarian pulled her bulky coat tightly around her torso. In frustration she snarled at them, 'You two have fun then. Don't bother concerning yourselves with me.'

She slammed her door, spun around brusquely and stomped back down the road.

Anaïs watched her leave through the rear vision mirror until Prince obstructed her view.

'She's a bundle of laughs,' he quipped from the backseat.

Anaïs grinned. 'Yeah, she's a real pleasure to be around.'

Prince flashed her a smile. *'You can certainly pick them.'*

'I wish it was up to me. I don't think I'm in charge of the picking department. It's the other way around. Everyone seems to pick me.' She pulled her knees up and wrapped her arms around them. Wearily, she expelled air in a long, slow sigh. 'I'm really tired. Think I'll try to get some rest while she's gone.' She turned sideways in her seat and balance her head between the backrest and her knees.

'I'll keep watch,' said Prince.

'You do that,' murmured Anaïs and yawned.

Prince reached forward and stroked her head. Instantly he was thrown back in his seat.

~

There were lights everywhere. People were cheering. They surrounded him on all sides. He heard the drawl of his own voice graciously thanking them. He looked down at his body. He was clothed entirely in skin-tight black leather. An acoustic guitar rested on one leg. He stroked its strings.

'Thank you very much,' he heard himself say again. 'This one's for my little girl.'

He put down the guitar and picked up a silver microphone. He was surprised how heavy it was. A solid weight, its size disguised its true mass. Using the cable attached to it, he held it secure with one hand and let it roll around in the open palm of his other. The microphone felt like a weapon. He juggled it and threw it in the air. The cable tightly coiled around his hand like a stockman's whip and he used it to guide the microphone back to his hand.

His palms were sweaty. In fact, he felt wet all over, completely soaked in perspiration. The leather clung to his body and pulled at his skin when he moved. It was very hot. The lights beating down from above were intense. He squinted and peered out under their glow, trying to make out the crowd. He could see their bodies but their faces were totally obscured by the light.

Music began to play. A lush crescendo of orchestral strings. He heard himself begin to sing. The experience was odd. It was as if he was only sharing the body he possessed and had very little command over it. His body was a vehicle and he was a passenger on the inside looking out, along for the ride. He could only understand fragments of the text that was being sung. He was singing something about a light burning brighter.

He sensed his voice more than he heard it. It was beautiful. Warm. Rich. Powerful and sonorous. It rose from deep within his core. There was an almighty passion behind it. It drove him on, the voice a force unto itself. The fervour inside grew as he continued to sing. It cocooned him. It buoyed him. Lifted him up and released him. He felt an enormous sense of freedom. A flower petal spinning on the surface of water. He felt alive.

He tried to draw in a breath, but there was no air, not even a wisp of wind. He choked. Then his head began to swim. He couldn't focus anymore. The sweat on his brow ran down over his eyelids and obscured everything. The bright light remained but the crowd was gone. He was alone. In a white room. Its walls glistened. He felt himself falling.

Then he saw tiles. Neat, bleached squares of porcelain. They rushed up at him as he fell towards the floor. He felt a tremendous shot of jarring pain as his head connected with the tiles. His skull bounced once and struck the floor a second time. He grimaced. He tried to move but couldn't. Where previously he'd had some minor control over his body, he now had none. His corpse was limp and failed to respond to the signals he tried to send it. He exhaled, managing to expel a breath. He forced his chest to expand and sucked but nothing filled his lungs. Only emptiness.

A shroud of darkness descended. The last thing he saw, as everything faded to black, was mould growing on the underside of a bathtub.

ON TARGET

The blip had increased in size. They were very close to its source.

It had been a long drive and night had already fallen by the time they arrived on the coast of Cornwall. They had practically crossed the entire country from east to west in a day. Not only had they travelled a great distance but they had also moved into another climate zone.

The temperature hadn't risen a great deal but there was now no snow, only rain and wind. It whipped off the ocean and buffeted the car as they drove along the coastal road. The sea was inhospitable, choppy and rough. White peaks stood out on the crests of waves like the snow-decked hills they had left behind.

After leaving the farm they had skirted north around London. They followed directions provided by the promptuary. It was surprisingly good at avoiding traffic jams.

After the refuelling of the car, Anaïs and the

librarian had maintained a tense silence. Eventually, they both realised it was not healthy to harbour irritation. They had tentatively begun to make conversation and established a sort of uneasy truce. Prince sat for most the journey staring out the window and trying to be as inconspicuous as possible. The vision continued to haunt him and he vainly tried to make sense of it.

Anaïs and Immi had questioned why the Inquisitor had stopped following them, but the less they thought about it the better. They had to keep moving. They had discussed what they would do if they saw him again. They couldn't address that concern. Individually they hoped their good fortune would continue, although deep down they both knew it would eventually run out.

Prince didn't want to think about it and stayed out of the discussions. He didn't want to upset either of the women. He was fully dependant on both of them to get him to the source of the signal. He had no idea what secret it held but the guidance from the promptuary was the only real magic Anaïs possessed. He had to trust it, just as he had trusted her.

He hoped that, if and when it came to it, she would have the power to stand up to the stranger. He convinced himself that when the time came, her powers would be enough.

Lizard was not a big town. It was practically deserted as they pulled into the centre. The rain had turned to spray and the beam of the nearby lighthouse cut through it. The beam of light swept across the horizon and presented an eerie backdrop in the blackened sky behind the houses as they cruised through the village.

The librarian stopped the little car and turned to Anaïs. 'Now what?'

Anaïs consulted her promptuary. 'It's moving, but it's very close.'

'Ok, then we'll watch and wait,' said Immaculate Phlox. 'With any luck it will find us.'

The light from the promptuary was the only light in the car. It lit up Anaïs's face as she concentrated on it. The librarian leant over her, trying to make out an image on the screen, but only Anaïs could read the contents of her own handbook. Even Prince leant over the seat. He studied the face of the small girl for a sign. The three of them huddled around the little book as if it was a campfire. Under the canopy of the stormy darkness it provided some comfort. It flickered on their faces like candlelight.

Anaïs suddenly stopped breathing. She held her breath for an extraordinarily long time and then slowly exhaled. She looked up, leant forward in her seat and wiped the condensation from the windscreen.

'There,' she said.

They followed her line of sight. A car had stopped on the opposite side of the road. A woman got out and popped an umbrella. She fought to stop it flying away in the wind.

Anaïs looked down at the handbook and then out the window.

'It's her,' she said.

The force that stuck the rear of the Morris Minor

spun it in a complete circle. As it turned, the little car careened across the wet, slippery road in a direct trajectory towards the woman. She dropped her umbrella and flattened herself against her own vehicle as the Morris Minor slewed past her. It bounced off a high gutter further down the road, snapping its axle in the process. Its occupants were thrown around inside like dice in a cup. It crashed back down onto the cobblestoned street, lost its momentum and slid slowly to stop against another parked car. Its one remaining headlight lit up where it had come from.

On one side of the road the woman looked down at the crushed umbrella at her feet. She was shaking all over and clasped her chest to calm her beating heart. On the other side, where the Morris Minor had stood, was a new but beaten-up four-wheel-drive. One of its front fenders had been completely ripped off and there was an enormous dent in the bodywork where it had connected with the tractor. A large dog scrabbled through its broken windscreen and perched itself on the bonnet. Even with the noise of the wind its claws could still be heard scraping on the metal. The rain fell like a heavy curtain.

CAPTURED

P rince was pinned with his back to the wall. The massive hound had its paws on his chest, its hot breath on his face. Prince could feel it blasting his features like a hot-air gun. And he could smell it, the stench of death.

Anaïs was shocked. The whole time she had thought the man and his dog were after her. It now seemed that their goal had always been Prince.

The damaged rear door of the Morris Minor had fallen off when the car had come to rest. It had been all too much for the old vehicle. Its front bumper rested on the ground, its axle broken from the impact with the gutter. It pulled a sad face with its crumpled grill.

The hound had launched itself from the bonnet of the four-wheel-drive and bounded across the road towards them, its sharp claws clattering on the cobblestones. Anaïs had watched in horror as it had dragged Prince from the back seat of their vehicle like a ragdoll. Prince had landed on top of the dog as they crashed to the ground beside the car. The impact caused the dog to involuntarily release its grip on him. Prince had managed to shake himself loose and sprint across the road. The dog had untangled its legs and charged after him. It quickly caught up to Prince and used the weight of its body to throw the shade off balance. Prince had been spun around, stumbled backwards and fallen heavily against the ancient stone wall of a house. Before he could recover, the dog had stood erect on its hind legs and used its considerable mass to press the shade hard up against the wall.

As the dog dug its claws deeper into Prince's chest, his disguise flickered and dematerialised, revealing the real him. He turned his face to one side and pulled it away in an effort to keep it out of reach of the hound's sharp fangs. They dripped with steaming saliva.

The dog's claws drove into his chest like needles. He could feel every one of them. In fact, he could feel everything. It had been a long time since he had felt pain. Now it was there, it was excruciating. He felt the entire weight of the animal pressing against him. Had it been necessary for him to breathe, its sheer bulk would have prevented him from filling his lungs.

Anaïs watched helplessly as the Inquisitor extracted himself from his damaged vehicle and march purposely across the road. The wind tugged at his long coat. The rain was heavy now and beat down on his bald head. It ran in rivulets over his shaved skull and down his face. He blinked to clear his eyes.

In his left hand he held a scarlet book and was loudly reciting words from it in a foreign language. He held his right hand high above his head, as if he was about to bring it down like the blade of a guillotine. As he approached the dog and its prey, his words increased in volume.

Out of the corner of her eye, Anaïs noticed her promptuary flashing. It lay on the floor in front her. Its bright, blinking light filled the interior of the car. For the moment she ignored it and strained to hear what the Inquisitor was saying. She looked around the car for a way to get out. She was unhurt but pinned in her seat by the dashboard and collapsed front end of the vehicle. Its windscreen had shattered and shards of glass lay scattered over her and the librarian. They glinted in the winking light of the promptuary. The librarian lay next to her, slumped over the steering wheel. There was a long gash across her temple. She was alive but her breathing was shallow.

Anaïs fought to free herself. It was pointless; her arms were trapped between the seat and the dashboard. She wiggled her fingers and tried to force one arm down to the floor. The promptuary was tantalisingly close. Her fingertips clawed at the rubber mat on the floor, centimetres from the book. She willed it to come to her. It refused to cooperate.

'Come to me!' she cried.

With her command the promptuary obliged and began to creep across the floor towards her hand. It reached the edge of the rubber mat but this prevented the book from moving further. Exasperated, Anaïs huffed, 'C'mon, you stupid thing. What's your problem?'

There was no further response from the book except for its blinking. Frustrated, Anaïs gave up and sank back in her seat. She peered through the broken remains of the windscreen.

The ferocity of the storm outside had increased. A fierce wind sent the rain hurtling horizontally through the air. Then something landed in the middle of the street, obscuring her view of the three figures up against the wall.

Dressed entirely in black, it was wrapped tightly in a long coat which fanned out from its hips. It wore a wide-brimmed fedora. It, too, held a book in its hands. Like the promptuary it emitted bright light, only it was far brighter. The slender figure held the book open with both hands and pointed it directly at the figures against the wall. Anaïs watched as the dark figure stiffened and braced its body against the handbook.

There was a dull, muffled whump. Anaïs felt the pressure of an implosion suck in around her like a blanket. Everything in the street that wasn't bolted down lift about a metre into the air. The Morris Minor did the same. Everything hovered and held its levitated position. Even the drops of rain stopped falling and froze in mid-air as gravity failed to have an impact on them.

A narrow beam of light streamed from book. It cut a horizontal line across the street, pierced the dog and reflected off the animal, hitting the Inquisitor. The beast took its attention off Prince and directed it towards the figure with the book. It snarled and howled, throwing its head back in what appeared to be anguish. Apart from its head the rest of its body was frozen to the spot. Anaïs watched its muscles flex but fail to provide movement. The Inquisitor also appeared to be pinned to the spot by the light. The only movement came from his eyeballs which rolled around in their sockets in fear.

Slowly, they were both completely enveloped in a vortex of light. It began to consume them. A low droning built until it was a high-pitched squeal. Anaïs writhed in her seat, wishing she could clamp her hands tightly around her ears. The sound pierced her eardrums.

The light around the Inquisitor and his dog grew brighter. Between them, at its core, a pure-white ball of intense luminosity formed. It crackled loudly, competing with the din of the high squeal. Its glow lit up the entire street. Prince tried to pull his head away from the source but was hampered by the wall behind him. He pressed his head against it, squeezed his eyes shut and gritted his teeth.

First the hound, and then the Inquisitor, began to melt from view in the brilliant light. Their bodies became transparent. Their features faded until there was just a faint outline in the form of a silhouette. The light then swallowed them and they disappeared altogether.

The figure in the middle of the street fought frantically with the book. It strained against it and Anaïs watched it struggle to maintain its footing. With great effort and a loud cry it slammed the book shut. In an instant the light was extinguished. Everything that had hung in the air slammed back to the ground.

The impact of the Morris Minor hitting the ground took the wind out of Anaïs. The piercing squeal suddenly ceased, leaving a ringing in her ears. She sank back in her seat, gasping for breath. She closed her eyes, attempted to regulate her breathing and tried to clear her head. The painful ringing in her ears slowly abated. It was replaced with the sound of rain drops gently slapping the thin metal roof of the Morris Minor.

AN INTERVENTION

P rince released the tension in his corpse. He slid down the wall and slumped to the ground. He reached up and gingerly touched the features of his face to make sure everything was still in place. Leaning forward, he wiped the dog spittle from his cheek with the tail of his shirt. He still felt lingering pinpricks in his chest where the hound's sharp claws had been. He flattened his back against the wall and looked down at his body.

Was that blood on his shirt?

There were definitely dark patches where the dog's claws had pierced the material. He touched the spots with his fingers and winced. He massaged his chest and it eased the discomfort. Heat and pain were sensations he had long forgotten. Now they were palpable and real. He almost felt alive.

He looked around the street. Across the road and to his left the four-wheel-drive hissed steam from its cracked radiator. To his right the Morris Minor looked sad and totally defeated. It sagged on its collapsed front end. Neither vehicle was going anywhere. Prince watched as the tall figure in black moved towards the small car. He pulled up his legs and attempted to stand, but with every movement his chest burned. The pain was just too much. He slumped back against the wall.

He owed Anaïs some protection. It troubled him that he couldn't move and again he strained to get up. His body failed to respond. He gave in, defeated. He was truly spent. Somehow the beast had drained him of energy. There was nothing he could do but wait.

For a moment he considered what had happened. The man and the dog had been after him all along. For some reason this mysterious entity had saved him, but to what end? Was it only so it could get to the little witch?

He shook the thoughts from his head and returned his focus to the street. He could just make out Anaïs through the shattered windscreen. Her face was lit up by a light coming from within the vehicle. Her eyes were fixed on the approaching figure. There was courage and tenacity in them. She wasn't giving up without a fight.

'Good, that's my girl. Give 'em hell.'

Only, he could see she was helpless, pinned inside the little car. Just like him she couldn't move. She couldn't defend herself. They were both helpless. He sensed his strength returning and tried to stand again. It wasn't enough to coax movement into his body. He grunted in frustration.

The figure stood calmly in front of the little car and opened its book again. It leafed through the pages, found what it was looking for and laid what appeared to be a piece of glistening, golden string along the spine. It closed the book and held it out in front of its body with both hands. With its thumb it pressed a large button in the form of a star on its front cover. Prince recognised the book; it was another promptuary.

A fresh beam of light shot from the book. Softer and less penetrating than the previous glow, it had a faint blue hue. It intensified and changed colour. A pencil-thin line of bright red ran through the centre of the beam, and, as it did, it spread to the outer edges. Blue became purple. The beam of light pierced its way across the street and, like its predecessor, completely engulfed its target. The Morris Minor changed colour. The metal bodywork itself became a light source and emitted an azure-blue glimmer before transforming into purple.

Anaïs struggled in her seat. The courage in her eyes had melted. A look of fear now twisted her visage.

He heard the sound of metal scraping on metal. It grated on his ears like a grinder. There was a popping and crunching noise and the front of the Morris Minor began to right itself. The bent grill and dented bumper-bar creaked back into shape. The bonnet lifted itself, the indentations in it sprung out and it returned to its smooth, pre-crash form. Prince watched in fascination as shards of glass spun up into the air and slotted themselves back into their original positions in the windscreen. They made a sound like an archer's arrow finding its mark over and over again. The front wheels, which had slumped at a rank angle, pulled themselves into an upright position. The second headlight came back to life. Its beam shot across the street and blinded him.

He raised his arm to shield his eyes. Tentatively he peered out from under it and slowly his eyes became accustomed to the light. Though the righted windscreen Prince had a better view of Anaïs. She was now free to move. But she didn't. Her hands were on the dashboard and she was frozen to the spot, her eyes locked on the concealed face of the figure. Strangely, she was calm. Any hint of fear in her eyes had dissipated.

Prince turned his attention back to the figure in the middle of the street. The stream of light from the book diffused and receded back into it. The figure adjusted its stance. Spreading its legs apart it locked its knees and lifted the book above its head with both hands. A bolt of lightning shot down from the heavens and hit the book squarely in the centre of its cover. The figure laboured under the impact, sinking to its knees with the force from above. Instinctively, Prince clamped his eyes shut. There was an enormous crack. The ground rippled, a wave of vibrations running through both earth and air. Prince felt a trill of static electricity run through his entire body, and then silence prevailed. There was only the barest whisper of a breeze.

Prince let his head settle back against the wall behind him. If he could have breathed he would have expelled a sigh of relief through his lips. He opened his eyes and blinked. The street was lifeless. The mysterious figure in the middle of the road had vanished.

Movement to one side caught his attention. From around the corner of the only other vehicle in the street a woman slowly got to her feet. She used the car to support herself. Turning, she looked straight at him. The Morris Minor's headlights lit up her face. He recognised it. It was the female version of the face he saw every time he looked at his own reflection.

DELIVERING THE MESSAGE

She looked exactly like the picture he'd had in his mind's eye. She had his strong chin and his eyes. Her countenance bore a familiar determination. They were so very much alike. There was even a distinctive curl to her lip just like his.

Thoughts of his youth came flowing back. It felt almost like yesterday. That was when he was himself, the real him. That was when he enjoyed making music. That was when he had been so creative. Back then the world lay undiscovered before him. He was still free to shape it in his own way.

More memories came flooding back. He pondered where he had gone wrong. He had let them take him on the ride. He had gone along with all of it and given himself completely over to them. They had moulded him, contorted him into something he really wasn't. He had given up all control and become what they wanted. He had sold his soul. He had surrendered the only part of him which was truly him.

He saw that innocent version of him in her. The untainted part was strong. They were the same age, now, the age when he had died. Perhaps she was even a bit older. She was certainly in much better physical shape than he had been. She had taken good care of herself. She hadn't let the gatekeepers dictate her life. She still had it all in her own hands. She was cleverer than he had been. That part was from her mother. She had been smart as well. She had maintained her integrity. Somehow, with everything that had happened, she still had it. He had squandered his youth and so much more. It embarrassed him to think about what he had done to himself.

He closed his eyes. He thought back to when they had still been together. He saw himself sitting on the edge of her little bed. He was humming her to sleep. She held onto his index finger with her tiny hand. Her grip was vicelike. She squeezed so tightly it hurt. He marvelled that she already had such strength at her tender age. If he had left it up to her, she would never have let him go. He should have let her hold him, keep him there. He should have stayed. Had he done that he could be looking at her today through the eyes of a mortal.

It dawned on him that perhaps that had been his last lucid moment, sitting on the edge of a child's bed. Such an innocent place. After that the blizzard had hit. The world around him had gradually become snowed in. All remaining clarity had been lost. What followed was the beginning of a systematic decline into the shadows. Even in life, he had become a shade. Not long after leaving her bedside he had effectively died. It saddened him. The pain in his chest was no longer just from the hound's claws. It felt tight and heavy. He had chosen to follow the path of his own demise.

He recalled the moment in the back of the Morris Minor when he had been given the glimpse. He now knew what it had been. The '68 Special. Then he'd had the fame and could have made proper use of it. He should have gone back to his roots and stayed there. That night he had done that, returned to his core, the real him, and they had loved him for it. In retrospect, it had been the highlight of his career. He had done what was truly his own thing. This trait, this characteristic, this remarkable piece of him, buried deep inside, was what had made him special. It was what made him unique.

Unfortunately, he had squandered the moment like so many others. It had been his last opportunity. The final, genuine chance to redeem himself. After that his world had clouded over. It struck him again that if he had stayed true to himself, he might still be walking the planet as one of the living. And that now, he could be looking at his daughter with living eyes. Yet, he didn't dare open them for fear that she would no longer be there.

Was she still there?

'Dad?'

She was very close. He could feel her breath on his face. It was soft, warm and comforting, not like the harsh, furnace breath of the dog. The sensation was fantastic. He bathed in it.

The words formed in his mouth without thinking. He felt her hair play across his face and whispered in her ear. 'Buttonhead, I'm here darling.'

She caught her breath. 'Is it really you?'

'Yes.'

He opened his eyes and looked around. It took him a moment to realise where he was. He was standing. Anaïs held his right hand. She also held his daughter's hand. The three of them stood in a tight circle in the middle of the road. Practically the same spot where the mysterious figure had stood. *How did he get here?* The question came and went in an instant. He let it go.

The rain was still falling, but bounced off an invisible field surrounding them. Unseen energy flowed from the witch's hand along the full length of his arm. He felt it pulling on his tendons, yet the grip on own his hand was loose. The pull went further into his body. He felt it tugging at his chest; a white heat drawing a line deep into the centre of his being, encompassing his dormant heart. It was as if there was a hand firmly clasping it. The hand felt soft like a pillow, squeezing ever so gently. It felt as if the organ itself was detached from his body. It floated freely within the empty void of his soma. He felt incredibly vulnerable. He sensed that the force encompassing his heart could wrench it out at any moment. It was no longer his. He was nothing. He was not the one in control. Anaïs was. She was the conduit that joined them. This tiny waif held his existence in her hands. He gave himself over to her. If there was ever a moment when he had to utterly and completely trust the little witch, this was it.

'Dad?'

His daughter snapped him out of his physical concerns.

'What do you want, Dad? Why are you here?' Inquisitively, she tilted her head to one side. 'How are you here?'

He turned his full attention to her. She was of utmost importance now. She was the sole reason he was there. Nothing else mattered. Only his daughter. Only her.

He read her face. There were so many questions written on it. He had no answers. Pure emotion flooded him. He floated on it. His heart swelled and pushed against the force around it. He looked deep into her eyes. 'I just wanted to tell you I love you.'

She smiled. There was no longer a need for answers and an inner peace came over her. 'I love you too, Dad.'

He nodded slowly. 'I know. I've always known, honey. I wanted to say how sorry I am.'

She shook her head. 'There's no need. You don't have to do that.'

'Yes I do.' He bit his lip. 'I should have stayed. I should have kept my eye on you. I got distracted with all the wrong things.'

Her face twitched. 'It has been hard, Dad, but I'm ok.'

'I can see that. I'm proud of you, Buttonhead. Don't do what I did. Stay true to yourself.'

'Thanks, Dad, I will.' She choked on a tear. 'I am. It took me a while to realise it. I've made a few mistakes myself.'

'We all do,' he said. 'We have to. There's no other way to learn. Mistakes are good. Don't feel bad about them.' He paused and inhaled. It felt as if real air was flowing through his lungs. He practically choked on it. He cleared his throat. 'Just remember, there's only one you.' He studied her face. It was so beautiful. 'Your dreams matter, honey. Don't you ever give up on them.'

He paused. Coaxing his body to respond he commanded his hand to squeeze hers. He put pressure on Anaïs's hand and watched as in turn her other hand squeezed his daughter's. He looked her square in the face. Her eyelids fluttered and her eyes widened and locked onto his.

'I believe in you,' he said. 'And I always will.'

The pressure on his heart abruptly stopped. He had control over his body again. The force running through it ebbed and subsided. It was replaced with a different pull. Something more physical yanked down heavily on his arm.

The librarian was there. He hadn't even noticed her. His focus had been solely on his daughter. Immaculate Phlox had separated Anaïs from his daughter. She had broken the link, pulling them apart. The new tug on his arm was the physical weight of the little witch. She hung on in exhaustion.

FAREWELL

'*No!*'

'Dad?'

It was over, the connection broken. Anaïs was spent. She was pale as death. Prince's daughter stared down at the child. 'What happened?'

Anaïs's knees had gone on her and she sank to the ground. She panted, 'He's gone.'

'*No I'm not,*' said Prince.

Anaïs ignored him. It took all her energy to remain upright. She still held onto his arm for support. His daughter looked down at her.

'You don't look well. Are you ok?'

'No, not really,' said Anaïs timidly.

Immaculate Phlox intervened. 'She'll be ok.'

Prince's daughter was confused. She furrowed her brow and looked quizzically at the librarian. 'Do I know you?'

Anaïs reached into her pocket and pressed the star

button on the cover of her promptuary. She did her best to keep a straight face. 'No, I don't think so.'

'But, I thought I was just talking to my father.'

'Oh really?' said Anaïs. She looked up at Prince. 'Is this your father?'

The shade's camouflage had returned to cloak him. Behind it Prince was yelling and gesticulating. His daughter couldn't see any of it; neither could she hear him. From the moment the link had been broken, so had all forms of communication. His disguise was rock-solid. She only saw a middle-aged man staring at a fixed point somewhere in the distance. He didn't even appear to notice her standing right next to him.

His daughter knotted her brow and studied him carefully but he was totally unfamiliar. She was confused.

'No, I must have been mistaken,' she said. 'Unfortunately my father passed away many years ago.' She studied Prince again. 'Who is he?'

'Just a friend,' said Anaïs. 'We go out for a walk every now and then. It's good for him. It's a pity, but he can't speak and his eyesight is almost completely gone.'

The daughter looked at the old man with concern. 'Oh, that's sad.'

'Yes.'

Anaïs fumbled in her pocket and pressed the star again.

The woman's eyes glazed over. Her body stiffened.

'I have to get going,' she said.

'Yes, you do,' agreed Anaïs.

The woman cocked her head at Prince. 'Good luck with your friend.'

'Thank you,' said Anaïs. 'You have a nice evening.'

The woman's face lit up. 'You know what, I think I will.'

'Your car is over there,' said Anaïs and pointed towards it.

The woman looked around the street and scratched her forehead. 'Did we have an accident?'

Anaïs shook her head. 'No, just a close call. No damage done. Everyone's ok.'

'Oh good.' She smiled pleasantly at them. 'I'll be going. Nice to meet you.'

Anaïs nodded. 'Nice to meet you too, goodbye.'

'Goodbye.' She walked down the street towards her car.

Prince went to follow but Anaïs held him firmly with what little strength she still had. She gripped his arm with both hands and looked up at him.

'Let her go,' she said.

Prince let Anaïs hold him. She was right. He had to let his daughter go. There was nothing more he could do. Even more importantly, he realised there was nothing more he needed to do. A calm come over him. He dropped his shoulders and let his arms hang loosely at his side. He allowed the feeling to sweep through him. He basked in this new-found knowledge.

He was finished. He had done what was required.

He had achieved what he was supposed to do. He had delivered his message. And he was certain it had been received. For that he was eternally grateful to the little witch.

His daughter walked the last few paces across the road to her car. She turned and gave Anaïs a friendly wave before getting into the vehicle and closing the door behind her. She fumbled with her keys, inserted them into the ignition and started the car. The vehicle pulled out from the kerb and drove past them down the street. Prince watched its tail lights recede in the distance. Tears blurred his vision. The car's orange lights floated through them. The pinpoints of light swirled and morphed into an image: his daughter's face.

Now he finally had this clear snapshot of her, he held it firmly and silently vowed never to forget it. He rubbed his eyes and wiped away the tears. He looked around him and appraised the street. The librarian had left them and was walking back to the Morris Minor. The cracked radiator from the four-wheel-drive had stopped hissing. Even the wind had subsided and the rain had stopped. Anaïs lead him across the street and back onto the footpath.

As they walked, he thought about what the little witch had done. She had given him a truly wonderful gift. He felt compelled to return the favour. He had to repay her and give her something. He owed her. But what could that be? Was there anything he could do? He had nothing. He was dead. Even if he had something to give her, it couldn't be physical. Or could it?

Maybe there was some other way to help Anaïs. He

would have to start by working out what she really needed. There had to be something which was supremely important to her. Something special. Something which could convey the same sense of joy and fulfilment he was now experiencing.

He thought back over their conversations and everything that had happened. Then it occurred to him. There was something. It was complicated but he had to find a solution. Anaïs desired it above all else.

A WORD

'Purple,' said Prince.

Anaïs couldn't believe her ears. He talked and she heard him. Not a voice in her head but a real, physical one.

It sparked some motherly instinct in her. It also brought back a flood of personal memories. As a child she had great difficulty learning to speak. She still didn't know what had prevented her from doing it. It was as if an invisible barrier, or lock, was thrown around her vocal cords. Nan had thought at first she was under a spell. After a while Nan had discounted the idea and proceeded to try a few earthly potions of her own. Nothing worked. Nan didn't have a witch's talents. Anaïs remained silent.

Then one day her lips formed a word. She was as surprised as Nan. Their shock quickly transformed into joy.

When Prince spoke it was as if she were standing in Nan's shoes. Had she also turned a corner? A fine memory of Nan was something she could cherish. She was overjoyed. She was also relieved. It had been a trial dealing with a voice in her head that could come and go at will. Finally being able to talk on such a human level was marvellous. She stood there and grinned up at him. He smiled back.

'What did you say?'

'Purple,' said Prince. 'You like purple.'

'Yes I do, but don't worry about that. It doesn't matter. I can hear your voice.' She pointed at her mouth. 'From here.' She tapped the side of her skull. 'And not here.'

His eyes widened. 'Really?'

'Yes,' she said. 'And not only that, I can see you, the real you.'

'No camouflage?'

'No camouflage,' she said.

'Wow!'

Tears welled in his eyes. He held them back but one managed to escape and a single teardrop ran down his cheek. It made its way along his jawbone until it reached his chin. It then dropped off and slapped the ground between her feet. He ran the back of his sleeve under his nose and brushed the wetness on his chin away with the palm of his hand. He sniffed and puffed out his chest.

'Does that mean I'm back in the real world?'

'I don't think so. As far as I know we witches can't raise the dead.'

He was disappointed. 'Oh.'

'But something has definitely changed,' said Anaïs. 'I just don't know what it is, or what it means for you.'

He sighed and considered her for a moment. He straightened his jacket, smoothing it down carefully.

'No matter. I think it's about time we made this official.' He extended his right hand to her. 'It's a pleasure to make your acquaintance, Anaïs, or should that be Miss Purple,' he said and winked at her.

She beamed up at him. 'No, Anaïs is fine. But if you're set on formalities, I would prefer Miss Thistle.' She took his hand, lifted the edge of an imaginary skirt and feigned a curtsey. 'The pleasure is all mine.'

'Oh no, I think the pleasure is all mine. I may have found a solution to your problem,' he said.

'Really?'

He reached into the inside pocket of his jacket and produced a pair of sunglasses. They had a heavy metal frame. The lenses were teardrop-shaped and oversized. They looked very familiar. The style was special. She was sure she had seen them before. He folded the arms out and held the glasses in the light of the Morris Minor's headlights. He squinted through the coloured lenses to check if they were clean. He meticulously polished one lens with his shirt-tail and then carefully set the glasses on her face. He stepped back to admire her new look.

They slid down her nose and didn't hook well over ears. He took them off and bent the metal at the bridge. He then placed them back on her head. They still swam on her skull but now wrapped more snuggly around it.

'They're a little big but I'm sure you'll grow into them,' said Prince.

Anaïs was astounded. Everything had changed colour. Her entire world had become purple.

'I've been carrying them around forever and no longer have any use for them.' He put a hand on her shoulder. 'I would really like you to have them.'

'Thank you, Prince.'

He squared himself up. 'One more thing. If we're being formal about names, do you mind not calling me Prince anymore?'

'Why?'

'Because it's not my name. I now know what it is and a prince is not strictly what I am. When I was alive people called me the king. But even that title is not entirely correct.'

Anaïs was curious. 'Oh? And who are you, then?'

'My real name is Elvis,' said Elvis.

She studied his face for a moment.

'You mean *the* Elvis?'

He screwed up his top lip and swung his hips to one side. 'Yes, I'm afraid so. The one and only.'

Anaïs couldn't contain herself and jumped on the spot. 'That's so cool!' She cleared her throat. 'I'm sorry I didn't recognise you. You look so different in the flesh, in real life.'

'I know. I let myself go a bit.'

'That's an understatement.'

Anaïs beamed at him. Then her excitement waned. Something had changed about him. There seemed to be less of him. He was fading.

His hand on her shoulder lost its weight.

A sadness descended on his face. 'I think I have to go.'

'No,' she squeaked.

'Yes. I wish I could stay but I don't think I have a choice. As with most things, there's usually a price to pay.' His voice wavered and he cleared his throat. 'But before I go, I want to thank you from the bottom of my heart. You have made me complete.'

He raised his free hand to his breast. The one on her shoulder dropped down through her body and came to rest at his side. He was now virtually transparent and barely visible.

A woman pushing a pram came around the corner further down the street and walked along the footpath towards them. The pram was antique, dating from the 1950s. It was huge, with big wheels, carriage springs and a large, navy-blue canopy. She slowed as she approached Anaïs, acknowledging the little witch with a nod. She then turned her attention back to the baby in the pram. Anaïs heard it let out a small, sharp cry. She stepped back to allow the woman and pram to pass.

Elvis stood forlornly in the centre of the footpath and reached out a hand to Anaïs. The woman continued walking past Anaïs and collided with Elvis. 'Collided' is not entirely correct; she walked straight through what was left of the shade. The baby in the pram bleated. In an instant Elvis disappeared.

Anaïs was stunned. She stared blankly at the spot where he had stood. Her vision blurred as tears welled in her eyes. Was that it? It was so sudden. No goodbyes; no fare-thee-wells; no until-we-meet-agains. She had wanted to thank him for the sunglasses. Thank him for saving her. Thank him for just being there when there had been no one else. She felt empty inside and somehow betrayed. All that effort and then nothing. He was gone.

She looked up from the footpath, wiped the tears from her eyes and turned to go after the woman with the pram. The street was empty. She too had disappeared.

A GOOD SPELL

naïs stood despondently on the footpath and surveyed the street around her. Now that the rain had stopped, there was only the sporadic sound of individual droplets falling from the leaves of overhanging trees. Drip. Drip. The street was barren except for the wreck of the four-wheel-drive and the little Morris Minor. The librarian stood next to the car and waved her to come over. Anaïs signalled to her that she should wait. She needed a moment to herself. The librarian let out an exasperated sigh, pulled the driver's door open and slid into the car.

Anaïs took off the sunglasses and examined them. She had completely forgotten about her struggle with purple. Before Elvis had come along she had been obsessed with it. She had turned the world upside down trying to solve her problem. She realised now the problem couldn't be solved on the outside. All along it sat inside her. She had to change.

The world wouldn't completely alter itself for her.

She could influence her immediate surroundings. That influence was incredibly powerful and could have far reaching effects. She had seen how disastrous that could be. The repercussions of her actions had been huge. The knock-on effects were something she couldn't control. She had to be more careful and swore that she would learn how.

She was distraught with the knowledge she had only been successful at doing bad. In the past she had only focussed on what she wanted. It was wrong. It had caused pain and suffering and not brought her closer to her goal. She had been so fixated on doing it her way that she hadn't seen the correct path. It had been right in front of her the entire time. Elvis had shown her this.

She needed to do good in the world. She hadn't been aware of it before, but now saw it had to be her primary drive. She had to focus on doing good. Why had it been so difficult to discover this? She wasn't stupid; maybe a little too self-absorbed, but definitely not an idiot.

She still wanted the change. The colour purple would always remain an obsession. Elvis's gift was wonderful but she would need the help of outside forces to achieve a complete transformation. The forces did not necessarily need to be bad. She just needed someone else with the power to cast the right incantation. Or someone who could teach her how to do it. She needed a good spell.

'Anaïs?'

The voice pulled her from her thoughts. A woman stood next to her. Without even looking closely, Anaïs immediately knew she was a shade. Only she was different. This shade was special. She sensed this shade had come for her and knew her intimately. It had a familiar scent, the strong, sweet smell of a field of wildflowers in full bloom. Anaïs looked up into the shade's face and her eyes widened. She was stunned.

For a moment, their pupils met. Deep orbs, which Anaïs knew all too well, exuded incredible warmth even in death. The shade sank to her knees and pulled the little witch snuggly to her breast. She practically squeezed the life out of her.

As the shade's arms closed around her, Anaïs let her mind go. All the concern and worry, the unanswered questions, were immaterial. They melted away. It didn't matter that the shade felt as cold as an iceberg, that no blood coursed through her veins, that no beat was heard from her heart. Only one thing mattered.

Anaïs was no longer alone. Nan was back.

SUNRISE

The librarian's impatience reached breaking point. She called from the car, 'Are you coming or not?'

Anaïs yelled back, 'Give me a minute, will you?'

She looked around the street. *Where had the night gone?* The faint glow of the sun rising was turning the sky from black to blue.

Anaïs trudged across the street, wrenched on the door of the Morris Minor and slid inside. She slumped in her seat and stared blankly in front of her. She was exhausted.

The librarian turned the ignition but there was no response from the Morris Minor. On the surface everything seemed to be back in its place, but Anaïs noted a subtle difference. The interior of the car was immaculate, as if it had just come off the production line. There was a fresh sheen to the dashboard. The linen lining the roof no longer had frayed edges, and the tear that had previously been above the driver's seat had disappeared. The seats themselves shone with their original buffed red leather. The tip of the gear stick was decorated with a brightly polished billiard ball, emblazoned with the number eight.

The librarian tried starting the car again. Nothing happened, not even the click of a spark failing to ignite a piston.

'Dead?' asked Anaïs.

'Maybe,' replied Immi. 'I'll have a look under the bonnet. There could be a loose connection somewhere. Perhaps whatever it did to the car was only superficial.'

'Perhaps, but I think *it* was a she,' said Anaïs.

'I'm sure you're right.' The librarian cracked open her door and turned in her seat. Extending her leg she placed one foot on the pavement. She spoke over her shoulder. 'But after everything that's happened I'm hesitant to take things at face value.'

Immi reached deep under the steering column and pulled a green lever, popping the bonnet. She sat up, leaned back, steadied her stiletto against the door and shoved it open. It didn't make a sound. Even the hinges no longer squeaked. She extracted herself from the vehicle, walked around to the front of the car and lifted the bonnet. Anaïs heard her tapping on various parts of the engine. The librarian closed the bonnet and got back in the vehicle.

'Well?' enquired Anaïs.

'Looks fine to me. Actually the whole thing is in pristine condition. Not that I saw what it looked like before. But what do I know? I'm a librarian, not a mechanic.' She turned the ignition. Still there was no response.

Anaïs's frustration got the better of her. She slammed her fists down on the dashboard. 'Start, why don't you!'

There was a minute ticking under the hood and then the engine roared to life.

The librarian shot Anaïs a sideways glance and shook her head. 'You've got to be kidding.'

Anaïs shrugged and grinned. 'Maybe it only listens to me.' The little witch directed her attention to the car. 'Sorry, I didn't mean to yell,' she said and caressed its dashboard.

The Morris Minor revved its engine, seemingly in response, before settling into a purring idle.

The librarian straightened in her seat. 'This is a rather fortunate development. Could you do this before?'

'Nope,' said Anaïs, shaking her head and screwing up her face.

'I guess we can get going then,' said Immi. 'Any idea where?'

Anaïs raised her shoulders. 'Dunno. Your guess is as good as mine. Let's just start by getting out of here.'

The librarian obliged and slotted the vehicle into gear. She pulled out from the curb and guided the little car down the street. The wet cobblestones glistened in the light of the rising sun. The librarian squinted in the glare and pulled a pair of sunglasses out of her coat. The frames were encrusted with fake precious stones and had little wings fanning out from the top edges. She hooked them over her ears. Combined with her big hair, she looked like a throwback to the late 1960s.

Anaïs smirked at her and pulled out her own sunglasses. As she placed them on her head, and their lenses slid down in front of her eyes, the world turned a comforting shade of purple.

At the end of the street the librarian attempted to make a right turn. The chrome-spoked steering wheel refused to budge. She grunted and wrenched at it but the wheel remained in a fixed position, guiding the car in a straight line. The gear lever popped out of first and slotted itself into fourth. The Morris Minor shuddered. Its engine whined, labouring for a moment under the strain, before winding itself up. A low whir grew steadily, running up through the frequencies before emitting a high-pitched squeal. Vibrations ran through the vehicle's bodywork. Its metal panelling sang in tune with the sound of the motor.

The car radio sprung to life. It squelched loudly. The needle shot backwards and forwards across the dial before stopping. The bombastic, slow rock tones of Queen's 'I'm in Love with My Car' rose in volume, drowning out the engine and filling the cabin.

The Morris Minor engaged its clutch and shot forward, pinning them to the backs of their seats. A look of panic flashed across their faces and the eyes of both the librarian and the little witch widened. The occupants of the vehicle grasped the edges of their seats and watched the tight, hedge-lined road ahead zip past them in a blur.

Thank you for taking the time to read *Thistle Witch.*

All authors appreciate knowing what you think about their work. Posting a review and other feedback helps improve their writing, assists readers in discovering their work, and is generally accepted as good karma.

Please consider **posting an honest review** on the web store where you purchased this book, or on Goodreads.

Word of mouth is an author's best friend, and much appreciated.

Anaïs's adventures continues in

Discovering Magic: Anaïs Blue Book Two.

The witch is back.

Anaïs Blue continues her complicated quest. Not only does she have a steep supernatural learning curve, but all is not right with the universe.

Catastrophes of a worldly and otherworldly nature. Trains, planes and enchanted automobiles. Shades, hellhounds and evil entities.

And if that wasn't enough, what are you to do when the most powerful magic you have goes haywire?

Nobody said being a witch would be easy.

Join Anaïs as she embarks on the next riveting phase of her mystical magic tour. She needs all the support she can get.

ISBN: 9789492523211

ALSO BY P J WHITTLESEA

One man. No future. A rich heritage.

Indigenous urbanite Billy knows very little about his ancestry. He is quite content to let it stay that way. One late night out changes all that.

Stranded on a central Australian highway with only the stars and mosquitoes for company, he finds his future determined by a pair of unlikely saviours. And a mysterious supernatural entity.

In an effort to get home Billy embarks on a surreal odyssey. Not only into his heritage, but also into himself.

Read his remarkable story today.

ISBN: 9789492523006

ABOUT THE AUTHOR

P. J. Whittlesea is an author and singer-songwriter. Originally from Australia, he now resides in Amsterdam in The Netherlands.

To find out about new releases, promotions, special sneak peaks, and to follow his writer's journey, sign up to the author's **book club**.

Scan the QR code below for access.

As a special introduction you will receive a free digital copy of:
The City of Shades: Anaïs Blue Prequel.

Lightning Source UK Ltd.
Milton Keynes UK
UKHW040835270223
417720UK00005B/1009